SORROW'S LIE

SORROW'S LIE

DANIELLE DEVOR

CITY OWL
PRESS

SORROW'S LIE
The Marker Chronicles: Book Four

CITY OWL PRESS
www.cityowlpress.com

Cover Design by MiblArt

Edited by Tina Moss

For information on subsidiary rights, please contact the publisher at info@cityowlpress.com.

Paperback Edition ISBN: 978-1-944728-41-0
Digital Edition ISBN: 978-1-944728-42-7

Printed in the United States of America

 CITY OWL PRESS
Escape Your World • Get Lost in Ours

ALSO BY DANIELLE DEVOR

The Marker Chronicles

Sorrow's Point

Sorrow's Edge

Sorrow's Turn

Sorrow's Lie

Sorrow's Fall

Tail of the Devil

The Devil's Liege

Constructing Marcus

Dancing with a Dead Horse

Strange Darkness

Anthologies

The Dark Dozen

Love Potion #9

PRAISE FOR DANIELLE DEVOR

"DeVor weaves a clever plot and brings the reader a huge mixture of emotions such as fear, anxiety, wonderment and complete shock." — *Lilian Roberts, author of Arielle Immortal Awakening*

"*Sorrow's Point* is a great horror story read. For me, this harkens back to the books of my youth, where the mystery and the horror were the main characters." — *Rebecca Trogner, author of The Last Keeper's Daughter*

"*Sorrow's Point* by Danielle DeVor is a new take on *The Exorcist* and for me a much better read. The author has invoked pure spine-tingling flesh-crawling terror from every chilling page." — *Simon Okill, author of Murder Most Deadly*

"The thing I love most about Danielle DeVor's work is that she never takes the easy road. Her imagination seems boundless. Sure, there's horror, demons, ghosts, and a myriad of other spooky goings-on. But I've noticed that she likes to mess with her characters. A lot. And the reader is better for it. And speaking of roads, the entourage is now headed for Tombstone, Arizona, in *Sorrow's Edge*, where more ungodly things are brewing. Good luck, Jimmy!" —*Steven Ramirez, author of The Girl in the Mirror*

"Once again DeVor hits a home run with a novel that will capture your attention and steal your time. *Sorrow's Turn*, like the other two books in the series forces your attention away from the real world and directs it into DeVor's universe where exorcists fight the unseen world. DeVor's talent for storytelling comes alive on the printed page. Sorrow's Turn has a quick pace and DeVor's writing makes the novel an easy read that you can lose yourself in." — *Louann Carroll, author of Innocent Blood*

Jimmy Holiday, exorcist extraordinaire, is about to embark on his most unusual case yet—a baby that may be possessed by the demonic...or worse, a true demon spawn. The Order wants him to make sure it is a true case and not some hoax...or so they say.

When the full truth of the corruption within the Order comes to light, Jimmy must act. With a voudou woman who lives down the lane as an ally, Jimmy must fight for the life of this supernatural child, but at what cost?

For my mom,
Without her, I never would have found a love of books.

ONE

END OF THE BEGINNING

SOMETIMES, your day just sucked. It all started before light, when someone or something startled Isaac, the amazing cat, and he pissed on my head. I couldn't figure out what had happened at first. Then, I discovered the sewer system had backed up.

"Tabby?" I still couldn't believe I was doing what I was doing, but every now and then you have to get in the thick of it.

"What?" she called from upstairs.

I'd saved her the horror.

"Are you bringing me the plunger or not?" I tried not to gag from the smell.

"If you'd hold your horses, maybe I could get down to you and not break my neck." Her feet clunked on the wooden basement steps.

I shut up. She was getting close to chopping my head off. Right now, she was still trying to help me.

When she got within reach, her face screwed up and she whipped her hand over her nose. "Here."

I took the plunger from her and attacked the drain again. It burped. Then, I felt something bump into my boot. I screamed.

"What is wrong with you?" Tabby asked.

My face reddened. And I was embarrassed as hell that I

squealed all because of this. Guess it was a good thing she liked me. "Something touched my foot."

"Since I doubt there are unholy shit demons, I recommend you suck it up."

I laughed and swallowed my injured pride. "Call the utility board. I give up."

"Like I told you an hour ago?"

I sighed. "Love you."

She didn't say a word and headed back upstairs. I stared at the mess and wanted to cry.

After I discarded all the crappy water clothes, pulled myself together, and got a shower, I went downstairs to find Lucy watching yet another scary movie. Isaac sat beside her, ignoring me. They were watching some gore fest, but I was silently thankful it wasn't another exorcism flick.

"Do you ever get tired of these?" I asked her.

She glanced up at me. Her white dress flowed in stark contrast with my mustard yellow carpet. "Not really. They're more interesting than anything else."

I rocked back on my heels. "Don't you like other stuff?"

She shrugged. "SpongeBob is okay."

I laughed. Once again, worrying over nothing. I needed to get a grip. "Okay. Go back to your movie. Where's Doc, anyway?"

"Looking into something."

"Got it." I left the living room and went into the kitchen long enough to grab a soda out of my awesome green fridge. Then, I passed back through and headed outside. Tabby sat on the front stoop, waiting on the city services folks. Her red hair sparkled in the early morning sunlight. She looked like a goddess in jeans and a white shirt. I was too lucky.

"They say when they would be coming?" I asked.

She shook her head. "Soon. I don't know."

I plopped down next to her and put my arm around her shoulders. Spring had been slow to come to Virginia, but it was finally warm enough to be outside without a coat. I was thankful. I needed to feel more normal again, not closed in. "If they don't get here in time, go ahead to see the wedding planner. I'll deal with the shit brigade."

Tabby snorted. "As if you don't want to get out of it anyway."

"It's not like Doc can handle it. Never mind that he isn't here now." I scratched my arm and peered down the street. Nothing but birds.

"No, but Mom will be here in about a half-hour."

I took my arm back, put my elbows on my knees, and buried my head in my hands. "Just when I thought the day couldn't get any worse."

She swatted me on the arm.

Tabby's mother arrived about twenty minutes later. Her little blue Toyota pulled into my driveway next to the SUV. Her bleached blond hair was arranged in a bouffant cloud around her head. More than once, I wondered how Tabby came from this woman. She must take after her dad.

"At least the drive wasn't bad," Tabby's mom said.

"Hello, Betty." I waved at her.

She glared at me. "Hello."

Tabby hopped up. "Thanks for coming, Mama. We really appreciate it."

"And that cat of yours is secured?"

"I put him in the bedroom. He won't bother you."

I could hear Isaac meowing from upstairs. I didn't relish us letting him out later. He was pissed.

I watched Lucy creep upstairs. I knew she couldn't let Isaac out, so that wasn't even a thought. I was more concerned that Tabby's mom would notice that a TV was on upstairs. Lucy, undoubtedly, was going to her room.

Tabby led her into the house. I glanced down the street, begging for the utility company to arrive. But they didn't, and I was stuck going along. I sighed and went into the house to grab my wallet and keys. Luckily, I didn't encounter Tabby and her mom. Wandering outside again, I climbed into the driver's side of the SUV. Tabby came out a few minutes later and hugged her mom on the stoop, then headed toward the car. Things had gone so easily, I couldn't help but wonder if Tabby hadn't performed a little witch-a-roo to make things go so smoothly.

"Okay, are you ready?" Tabby asked as she hopped into the car.

"I feel more like I'm going to the gallows."

She swatted me again. "Stop."

"Yes, ma'am."

I sighed as I put the car in gear. She peered over at me and regarded me carefully. I think she was afraid I was going to go rogue and drive us to Mexico or something.

"Jimmy, seriously, it isn't going to be that bad. If we don't like her, we can interview someone else."

I sighed again. "Guess I don't understand why we even need a wedding planner."

She glanced at me out of the corner of her eye. "If you get a case, we aren't going to have time to deal with flowers, setting up the church, where the reception will be, and the cake. The idea is to let the wedding planner know our budget, what we like, and let her take care of the rest. That way, if all hell breaks loose, the wedding can still go on as planned.

"What happened to the 'simple wedding'?" I know my folks got married in a church. My mom's parents showed up. My dad's didn't. They had pieces of cake in the church basement. That was it. I didn't have any idea why in the world we needed something bigger than that, but I had a feeling if I said much more, I was going to get my ass kicked.

"These days, this is a simple wedding."

"God, help me." It slipped. But instead of getting my ass kicked, Tabby stared out the window. I had dodged a bullet.

The first thing I saw when we arrived at the wedding planner's office was the flowers. Now, don't get me wrong, I don't mind flowers as much as the next guy, but this—this was over the top. There were so many of them; they seemed to burst forth from the walls, the floors, and even the desk. They weren't any one color either. And they were artificial, otherwise that much pollen would have sent me into a bizarre allergy fit. Luckily, the chairs were open and free.

"I'm so sorry," the older woman said. Her hair was dyed black, and I could still see the crow's feet at the corners of her eyes underneath all the make-up. "I had to pick up flowers for a client."

Part of me was impressed by her dedication, but the other side was inwardly cringing as to why she dumped all the flowers in her office when she knew she had an appointment with new clients.

Tabby grinned. "Nice of you to go out of your way."

The woman smiled tiredly. "I try to do everything I can." She held out her hand toward Tabby. "Eliza Donahue."

Tabby took the offering. "Tabby Settle, and this is my fiancé," she pointed at me, "Jimmy Holiday."

"Nice to meet you," I said. I was hoping this would be over with as fast as possible, but it wasn't looking like luck was going to be on my side today.

"Please sit," she said and started opening drawers in her desk and pulling free colorful brochures.

Tabby and I sat in the chairs on the other side of her desk.

Every so often, Eliza would hand over a pamphlet. I let Tabby take them. This was her dog and pony show.

"We want a simple wedding," Tabby started.

Eliza leaned back and stopped pulling things from her files and closed up the drawer in her desk. "Then what do you need me for?"

I forced myself not to roll my eyes, but it was hard. I didn't like the attitude she was copping. "We have jobs that take us away from town a lot. That makes it hard. We need someone to do as much as possible."

She stared down her nose at me. "And what is it you do?"

I grinned. "I'm an exorcist."

"Really, Jimmy. Did you have to?"

We were walking to the car and I had to rush to keep up with her. I hadn't seen her this upset in a while, but I was willing to take the hit. I couldn't stand it anymore. It wasn't my fault the woman freaked. Granted, I could have probably put it in a better way, but I was done with her attitude.

"You do know she's the best in these parts?" Tabby threw open the car door and shut it hard after she climbed in.

I got back in on the driver's side. Whether she was the best or not, I didn't care. She was more about the money. That pissed me off. "I didn't like her attitude."

"Obviously."

I shifted in my seat to look at her. I didn't care that she was annoyed at me. I wasn't kissing that wedding planner's ass. "Listen, why don't we go to the justice of the peace?"

Tabby paused, and then sighed. "Because there is no point in me getting married unless it feels like it means something. A judge feels so sterile."

I would love to know where women come up with this stuff. My head was starting to pound. "Can you say you are comfortable with a minister either?"

"Like you'd be willing to have a handfasting." She seemed to curl in on herself.

"Why not?" Not that I knew what that was, but wedding stuff was not my forte.

She turned toward me. "You'd do that for me?"

Obviously, she didn't figure in that I was willing to die for her, but I'd forgive her for it. I'm not exactly vocal. "I want you to be happy. We don't need any wedding planners. We'll take our time. Make sure everything is taken care of. Then do this...whatever it is."

She swatted me on the arm.

"Besides, this way, Doc and Lucy will be able to participate."

She beamed. "I love you, ya goof."

"I love you too."

TWO

WELCOME TO THE UNIVERSE

THE MINUTE I pulled into the driveway, my phone rang. It couldn't have been any more perfect. I was starting to hate clichés. I jerked it from the cup holder. It was Father Martin.

"Yeah?"

I heard what sounded like him swallowing. "How fast can you get to National, Kentucky?"

"Since I don't know where National, Kentucky is, I can't say." I motioned for Tabby to go ahead. She shook her head.

Father chuckled. "That was pretty stupid of me, wasn't it?"

"Nah, just forgetful."

"There is something unusual going on there. And well, Rome must send their specialist here on a transatlantic flight to get them in on this matter. In the meantime, they would like a Marker there to check things out as soon as possible. Hopefully, today. You seem perfect for the job, considering you are used to the unusual."

That was putting it mildly. As far as I knew, I was the only guy to exorcize a corpse. "Okay. What is it I'm supposed to do?"

"Find out if there is a 'devil baby'."

I dropped the phone.

"Mr. Holiday?" The voice asked faintly from the speaker in the ear piece.

I picked it back up, my hand shaking. "Sorry. Just a shock."

"No matter at all. I will forward you the information you need. Can you leave now?"

I cleared my throat. Well, that put a monkey wrench in all our plans. "Give me time to get my mail held and get packed."

"That will do." I set my phone down in the cup holder and leaned in the seat.

"What is going on?" Tabby asked.

"I don't even know if you'll believe this one." I took a deep breath. "Let's get rid of your mother and I'll tell you all about it."

No way was I going to talk about this with the battle axe around. I didn't need all the snide comments about my mental state. Granted, I was not quite sane, but that woman could take anything and make it shameful. I was not a fan of hers.

Tabby smacked my arm, shook her head, and got out of the car. "Whatever you say."

I followed Tabby into the house. The discussion was not over, but I wasn't going to start it up again—especially around her mother.

She was standing inside the living room, glaring at us. "I don't know how you can stand living with that thing. All it did the entire time I was here was make noise."

Tabby sighed. "Did you try talking to him?"

"Now, why would I do that?"

I wanted to slap the woman. Nothing with her was ever easy, but she couldn't let anything go.

I glanced up the stairs to see the usual ghost. Lucy, my six-year-old spirit, was standing there with her hand over her mouth as if to try to keep from giggling. I winked at her.

"It could have been worse, I guess, except for the stink," her mom said, then looked me up and down as if I was dirt under her shoe or something.

I wasn't about to have someone insult me in my own damn

house. "How would you know? I'm surprised you can smell anything over the top of that cheap perfume you insist on wearing."

"Well, I never." She huffed, put her head in the air, and walked out of the house. Tabby followed her, trying to calm her down, but the woman hopped right into her car and took off.

Once Tabby got back inside, she fumed. "Jimmy, did you have to?"

"I absolutely did."

"You couldn't have held it together for five minutes?"

I shook my head. "Nope. I get that she hates my guts, but I'm not taking shit from her. She could have been decent about the whole thing, but she wasn't."

"And where does that leave us?"

I shrugged. "There's no chance we can count on her to help watch out for workmen in the future. I'd honestly rather not have her in my house. Besides, there are more things to worry about than your mom's hurt feelings."

"You really make things difficult sometimes, you know that?"

I pulled her into a hug. "Sorry." I motioned for Lucy to come down. "Why don't you go let the slobbering beast free?"

Tabby laughed. "Oh no, buddy. You go let him out. I'll hang with Lucy."

I crept upstairs, dreading this one. While I knew he wasn't going to repeat this morning's performance, I would be fortunate if I didn't end up losing a bit of blood.

I opened the door to our bedroom and froze. My pillow was ripped apart, stuffing spread all over the bed and floor.

"You little shit!"

He appeared at my feet. Didn't walk. Appeared. And he was smiling.

"You are lucky I love you."

He rose up, rubbed against my legs, and left the room.

"Son of a bitch."

After I finished cleaning up the mess, I headed back downstairs. Tabby and Lucy looked at me and started to laugh.

"What?"

"You have cotton or something in your hair." Tabby guffawed.

I ran my hand through my hair and found the ball of fluff. "You can thank your brat of a familiar."

Isaac meowed from the back of the couch.

Tabby snickered. "Seriously, where are we going? Is this whole thing going to give me a headache?"

I walked over to the computer and booted it up. "Kentucky. Probably. Do me a favor and hose out the basement. I have to get our reservations."

She raised her eyebrow and gave me the glare of death. "How about I start packing for the both of us and you take care of the shit in the basement? Literally."

I sighed. "What? Isaac's little game wasn't enough?"

She snorted. "If we both go down, then we will still need to pack. If I pack while you hose, at least then you won't be cleaning up puke as well as shit and both things get done."

"All right. But next time, you're doing it."

She laughed. "I hope to God there isn't a next time."

I fiddled with the computer some more, avoiding the inevitable. When I finished, I noticed the receipt from the Utility Board sitting there in its yellow-ey goodness on the table. The guy had scribbled that the back-up was on them and not on me. So, no money was owed. Thank God. It meant I didn't owe Tabby's mom any money.

No sense in putting it off any longer. I laid down the receipt and walked into the hallway. I opened the door to the basement and gagged. The stench was as bad as the demonic. The dank staircase didn't help, but the smell was simply awful. I flipped on the light. The floor of the basement was not something I wanted to witness. I gagged again, then went outside, grabbed the water hose, dragged it with me into the house, and hooked it up to the kitchen faucet. I yanked it along with me downstairs.

"Okay, can we come around now?" Doc asked.

I laughed. "You might want to avoid this and watch TV with Lucy." Might as well save as many people as I could from the horror.

"I'll keep you company. Ain't got no smell."

It was nice of him. But then, Doc was always surprising me. Yet, what he said made me pause. Lucy had the ability to sort of smell things by letting them pass through her body. After she'd discovered that, I kind of figured they all could. "Really?"

"Not one bit. Never got the talent when I died. Lucy's special. Kind of miss not having something special. Not sure if it's because of the way I died or what. Some spirits can sense a lot more than I do."

"Not sure I'd want to run into those. You're pretty damn powerful." And he was, too. Managed to get things I never could have gotten my hands on without breaking fourteen million laws.

I began rinsing everything down the drain. It was a heck of a job. Truly, it was going to take a lot more than the hose to make this safe again. When we got back, I'd scrub the floor, but for now, it would be good enough. We didn't have time for more. "You know you're treading some might scary waters."

I peered up at Doc. His eyes seemed dark, but it could have been the shadow off his hat.

"What do you mean?" I asked.

"This thing. I've heard of 'em before. They ain't good."

"I'm only supposed to make sure it's real and then let the experts take over."

Doc chuckled. "Go ahead and believe that if you want to, but we all know that they ain't exactly trustworthy."

I scratched my head. Everything had worked out okay so far. I couldn't blame the Order for Tabby being possessed last time. There were a lot of factors at work there. "All I can do is the best I can."

He nodded. "Make sure you're careful. Those things are the devil in flesh. And they bite."

With a pop, he was gone. I presumed up with Lucy or something, not that it mattered. I had to get going. If I didn't get all this done, this trip to Kentucky was going to take a heck of a lot longer than I wanted. I finished with the basement and dragged the hose back upstairs.

"You done already?" Tabby asked from up above.

"With as much as I can right now. We'll do major cleaning when we get home."

Tabby lumbered down the stairs with both of our suitcases. I ran up a few steps and took them from her. "You should have told me. I would have helped."

"I'd much rather have the hose outside."

I set the suitcases on the floor, saluted her, and got rid of the hose. When I came back inside, Tabby was wiping up the floor with some cleaner where the wet hose had been.

"Sorry about that."

"Goes with the territory." She took the cleaner into the kitchen and then plopped onto the sofa.

I surveyed the room. Lucy was sitting in front of the TV, but looking at Tabby instead of the screen. In fact, the TV wasn't even turned on. That was unusual.

"You okay?" I asked Lucy.

"Uh-huh."

"So, what is all this about?" Tabby asked me. She seemed weary. Circles lay below her eyes.

I rested beside her. "Apparently, there is a devil baby or a demon baby in Kentucky. They want me to prove or debunk or something."

"That's not your area of expertise."

"You're telling me. Martin said they want me to take a preliminary look before the experts get there tomorrow."

Tabby groaned. "What did he say exactly?"

I paused. "He mumbled something about a transatlantic flight and asking how fast I can get there."

"Maybe the crap in the basement is some type of omen?"

I sighed. "I sure as hell hope not. Either way, I don't know if you should come."

She glared at me. "Because being separated from you worked so well last time?"

Yeah, it had been while I'd been in Italy that she'd been possessed. I was stupid. "No, you're right. I'll get my act together."

"For sure this time?"

I sighed. "Okay. I get it. Let's get ready."

"Let's."

THREE
OBLIVION

AFTER GETTING everyone loaded in the car, including Isaac, I slumped into the driver's seat. Granted, it would have been easier to take Isaac to a kennel, but as he'd shown before, he might come in handy. Besides, I liked the little booger.

It seemed like everything was telling me not to do this except my own ego. Maybe it was an impulse. I don't know what was preventing me from calling Father Martin back and telling him I'd changed my mind. I didn't know what I was doing. I had no manual or encyclopedia of creatures to compare the kid. That left me with what I knew about devil babies coming from movies like *It's Alive*. Not an expert there. I wasn't even sure if I could debunk it, unless a fake horn fell off or something.

"Are we going or what?" Tabby asked suddenly.

"Huh?"

"You've been sitting there for like five minutes."

I shook myself awake and chuckled sadly. "It's been a long day, and it isn't even noon."

"Sure you don't want me to drive?"

I sighed. "I'll be okay for now. I'll let you know if you need to take over."

"Okay. As long as you're sure."

I nodded and started the car. Lucy and Doc were in the back seat with Isaac between them in his cat carrier. One big happy family. As the miles ticked away down the road, more and more a feeling of dread that I couldn't ignore crept over me. And when the giant rainstorm hit, I'd had enough.

"Fuck this." I pulled into the nearest gas station and into a parking spot. I glanced in the rear view mirror. "Okay, Lucy, lay it on me. Is this going to be bad?"

She nodded.

"Worse than last time?"

She glanced at Doc, then back at me. "I don't know."

I looked at Doc in the mirror. He shrugged his shoulders.

"Lots of help you guys are."

Lucy barely smiled. Now, that was a bad sign.

"Okay. I'm gonna get screwed, aren't I?"

Tabby sighed. "Probably. And I could say I told you so, but it took someone with more power than me to hit you over the head with a frying pan."

"Hey, I never said I was smart." I drummed my fingers against the steering wheel as the rain drummed against the roof of the car. Since I had already agreed to do this, I was kind of at a loss. "So what do I do?"

"Not much you can do except what you promised. But when it all goes to hell, tell them about it. They will keep giving you these assignments as long as you let them."

"Or as long as whoever is giving me a bad name keeps it up."

"That too."

I scratched my chin. "That's one thing I don't understand. I've never even met any of these guys in person. How in the hell did I get an enemy?"

"Don't take much," Doc said. "Sometimes, it can be as simple as somebody not liking the look of your face. Men been shot dead for less."

The rain started to let up. But as usual, Doc was right. I didn't like thinking that I was possibly walking into a viper pit.

Though, if I were honest, it would better to know what I was facing than be surprised all to hell. "Guess that's our cue."

Tabby chuckled.

I drove straight through to the address I was given. The sun was bright in the sky again. The storms had moved on. It was only a little past noon, so if things went right, we could be heading back home tonight. To be honest, I wished I could have left Doc and Lucy at home, but that wasn't an option either. It would have been safer for them, but Lucy could not be that far away from me. Since her soul was tied to me for energy, she was kind of my permanent sidekick. Besides, the less time I spent in Kentucky the better. It wasn't like I had a huge role anyway. I was supposed to see if this was a real devil baby. That was it, and from what I figured they looked like, wouldn't take much to find out if it was legit or not. Unless they pulled something elaborate. The more I thought about it, it would be hard to put makeup on a baby and not have it destroyed in a nanosecond. Babies are squirmy and rub against things and scratch things that itch even when you tell them not to.

We pulled up into this holler of a place. Sort of up the side of a mountain with a swatch cut through it. Small farms dotted the hills, but the road was a narrow bit of bare dirt. The grass had been mowed relatively recently. Some of the farms had old rusted equipment next to them. Others were completely well kept and looked like a woodsy paradise.

It was interesting.

"At least these houses are in okay shape," Tabby muttered.

Our last case had been in a place that was falling in on itself. The porch steps had given way from rot when we'd walked on them. It was not the type of structure you'd expect people to actually live in. But they had. And it worried me that people had to live like that. Especially when there was so much money in the country. In contrast, these houses—while weather beaten and old—were in good upkeep and the porches were sturdy. You could tell very few of these people had any money to speak of, but they took care of what they had.

"Jimmy, stop."

I slammed on the brakes. There, in the middle of the road, stood a slender old man with a scowl on his face. He wore blue pants and gray suspenders over a white cotton T-shirt. He glared at us for a moment, and then walked around to the driver's side. He waited for me to roll down the window. His face was a little scraggly as if he hadn't shaved in a couple of days. "You looking for the Devil House?" he asked, spitting a wad of tobacco juice on the ground.

I'd be lying if I said I wasn't shocked. Not every day someone normal talks about this stuff, let alone about the very thing I was supposed to investigate. He didn't even know me. "Yes, sir."

"Go up the road a ways. Look for the house with the greens shutters at the top of the hill. Can't miss it."

It bothered me that he knew what we were looking for. Of course, maybe it was simply that they didn't get many strangers in these parts and he put it all together. "Thanks. We appreciate it."

He leaned forward with his head inside my window and motioned toward Tabby. "Be careful, missy. Bad things up there."

He smelled like crème d' menthe and tobacco.

"I will," she said.

He backed his head out and stepped away from the car. "Tell ole' Woody I said hi."

"And you are?" I asked.

He walked away without answering and disappeared around the side of the house next to the road.

"Well, that was different," Tabby said as I rolled up the window.

"This whole thing is different." I wasn't sure whether to be uneasy or go with it like usual. I followed the road like the old man had said. The path stopped right at the top not twenty feet from a green shuttered farmhouse. In the dim sunlight, we couldn't even tell if there were lights on. The paint was cracked in spots, but it was still workable. I'd seen much worse.

I shut off the car. "You coming?"

She didn't answer me. She stared at the house for a minute, then opened the door.

Suddenly, a sound like a pissed off animal pierced the silence of the hill. It was more of a snarl than a cry. I tried to find the source, but saw nothing. "What the fuck was that?"

"We'd better stay in the car," Doc said.

"Good idea," Tabby replied as she got out of the car.

I crawled free and shut the door quietly behind me. I still saw nothing but grass and trees. I had no idea where that sound had come from except...inside the house?

"This is your case, not mine." Tabby walked around the car and stood beside me.

I snorted. Then, I peered back into the car. "Doc, keep an eye on Lucy and Isaac. The minute something goes wrong out here, I want to know about it."

Doc tipped his hat at me. "You got it."

I took a deep breath. I wasn't sure I was ready for this, but what the heck? Guess it came with the territory.

Tabby took my hand. Hers was sweaty.

"You okay?" I asked.

"I'll be okay when this is over."

I felt the same, but I wanted to appear strong. Best that I didn't start visibly showing my trepidation. The woman in that house would zero in on it like a hawk—they always did.

I led Tabby up the steps, released her, and knocked on the door. The door was dark green and the paint cracked, but it wasn't peeling. This close up, the house did need a sprucing up.

"Go away!" a woman's voice yelled from inside the house. It sounded like a combination between a hag and a flightless bird.

"I'm not here to cause any harm," I said to the door. And I wasn't. That was a job for others.

"Fuck that. Why should I believe you?" the hag asked.

It was a damn good question. And one I had no answer for. But out of politeness, she could at least open the door and let me see her for Christ's sake. "Look, I'm here to investigate. Will you at least come out to the porch to talk? I have my friend with me. Heck, we'll even step off the porch if you want."

I heard some rustling, which was odd unless there was a ton of trash on the floor inside the house. Of course, that was always a possibility.

"You ain't from Child Protective Services?" The voice was louder now, like she was on the other side of the door.

"No, definitely not with them." Though I had to admit I wondered what a social worker would do if confronted with a real devil baby. Likely be something pretty damn entertaining.

She threw open the door and stepped onto the porch so fast, I didn't get more than a flash of green wall before the inside of the house was beyond my sight. I did see that there was not paper all over the floor. I guess that was a plus.

"All right. What you here for?" she asked.

"I'm here on behalf of the church to check on your son." Might as well be honest. It saved time.

Suddenly, she started cackling. "I'm sure you are, bucky boy. I'm sure you are." Then, she whipped her head in Tabby's direction. "And who are you?"

Tabby motioned with her chin. "His assistant."

The woman grunted, stared at us both once more, and then scurried back into the house so fast I couldn't even believe it. The door was slammed in my face.

"Well, there goes that," Tabby said.

I shook my head. I already knew it wasn't good enough. The Order would not accept, "The woman was mean to me and wouldn't let me in her house." It was a pickle. "If that's all it took, I'd have left Sorrow's Point long before I called you."

"Point taken. So what do you want to do now?"

I thought for a moment. There were no simple answers. And I didn't want to do half of the things that came to mind. "I guess I'd better try to chit chat with the locals some more and see if I can get any other information."

Tabby sighed, shielding her eyes from the sun and scanning the sky line. "How about her?"

I looked up. "Who?"

She pointed. "Her."

There was an old African American lady standing in the field near the house, staring at us. She wore a checkered cotton dress that seemed almost bleached from the sun.

"Can I help you?" Tabby called to her.

"You both better be getting away from there. Come on and have some coffee. I think it's about time you know what's going on around here." She put her hands on her hips.

"How do we get to your house?" I asked.

"Back out of there and turn left by that big old pine tree." She pointed with her finger then turned around and started walking. In a moment, she disappeared over the hill.

"Do we do what she said?" Tabby asked.

I shrugged. "Don't see anything else we can do. And hell, maybe we'll get a good story out of it."

Tabby rolled her eyes. "And maybe you'll get sucked in."

I put my arms around her shoulders. "That's what I have you for."

She pushed me away and got into the car. "Come on. Let's get this over with."

"Yes, ma'am." I hopped in and followed the older lady's directions.

Doc watched me through the rearview mirror. He didn't say anything, so I figured it was okay. Lucy was distracted, playing with Isaac in his carrier.

It wasn't hard to find the lady's house. It was the only one on that gravel road. The house was small and white, but well kept.

Several potted plants on the porch were bursting with flowers, cracking the pottery. The deck was a little gray, but seemed sturdy.

As soon as I stopped the car, Tabby hopped out.

"Isn't this beautiful?" She threw her hands into the air and grinned.

I got out carefully. Isaac meowed from the back seat.

"Shhh." I heard Lucy say to Isaac.

I gently closed the door and watched Tabby for a minute. Ever since she'd been possessed, I kept an eye on her anytime she did something that was unusual for her. Granted, flowers weren't all that weird. It was Tabby being this excited that had me worried.

The lady came out of her house. In her hands was a white dish towel. "Come on in, now. And tell those folks in the back they might as well come too."

"We have a cat. Is it okay if he comes inside?" Tabby asked.

The lady paused. "Not right now. But I'll get him some water."

"Thanks," Tabby said.

I froze. This woman was the second person I'd ever encountered who could see Lucy and Doc. It was kind of unsettling. And it was also interesting that she had an aversion to a cat in her house.

"We get to go inside?" Lucy asked.

I nodded. I had no reason for them not to except fear of the unknown, but the lady seemed nice enough. Might as well give Lucy joy where I could get it. Besides, between all of us, if something started to get weird, we could get out of there. The danger was pretty minimal.

The lady placed a saucer on the porch. Tabby got Isaac's carrier and let him out for a bit to do his business. He didn't run off, just went out in the yard, did what he needed to do, and trotted back. This was one case where we were lucky Isaac was unique. Tabby put him back in the carrier and added the water inside with him.

"Don't want to risk not being able to find him later," Tabby said.

"Good idea." Plus, I didn't want to have to defend him from nasty people...again. I shook off the memory. Not one I wanted to remember.

All of us followed the lady into the house. The first thing that stood out to me was the flooring. It was hardwood but so pale it looked bleached. The place smelled clean. It had been a very long time since I'd seen someone keep their home that nice. My mother sure as hell never did.

"Sit on down here and I'll get you that coffee. Shame the little one can't eat. I'd give her one of my cookies."

Lucy beamed. "I can still smell them."

The lady laughed. "Okay then. One cookie coming up."

She fiddled around the kitchen for a minute and in no time had us all arranged around her kitchen table with cups of coffee in front of us. Lucy was bouncing here and there. Too much excitement at being able to be seen by someone other than Tabby and me, I guessed.

"We never did catch your name," Tabby said.

"Lulu Woods. You can call me Woody." She lowered herself into her own chair gracefully after placing a plate with a cookie on it in front of the space in the table we'd made for Lucy.

Lucy crept in close and bowed her head over the plate.

"Woody, who was that old man in the road?" I asked. He also seemed nice enough, but there was something about him that didn't feel right.

"Ah, that's Charlie. He ain't no bother. Wanders once in a while when there's trouble on the hill. He's a fixture around here." She took a sip of coffee.

"Trouble follows that one," Doc said, pointing at me.

"Thanks a lot."

Woody laughed. "Trouble always follows those who can fight it. Has to do with maintaining the balance and all."

"What *is* going on over there?" I pointed toward the house on the top of the hill.

Woody leaned in close. "Mrs. Timberlake. That woman's a witch."

I watched Tabby stiffen.

"I'm not talking commune with forest spirits. That woman over there is pure evil. That devil baby is sure proof of it."

I blinked. "You mean it's real?"

"Real as you or I. She let the Devil give her a child. Bad juju all over."

Tabby readjusted in her seat. "What could she do with it?"

Woody coughed. "You keep messing with him and you're going to get to know the dark a lot more than you have already. Right now, you're a sitting duck."

Tabby twitched. "And what do you know about it?"

Woody leaned back in the chair and gave Tabby a measured look. "I know the old magic. Nature magic. Passed down to me from my mama. Don't get me wrong, I love God and Jesus. And I do my best to live my days by their rules, but sometimes you have to use the gifts you've been given. I've been having trouble with that one on the hill since she moved in. Can't keep milk products past three days because she curdles it."

"How is that possible?" I asked. Granted, I'd heard the old witch stories, but I never thought there would be any truth to them. The more I got sucked in, the more I started to learn how little I knew.

Tabby and Woody stared at me for a minute.

"Oh right. Magic. Sorry. The idiot will shut up now." I shuffled my feet against the floor.

"Anyway, a devil baby...they are bad business," Woody said. "Could be they plan to use it as a changeling. But I suspect far worse than that." She rubbed her hands up and down her arms as if she were cold.

I didn't like it. Woody, while having just met her, gave me the feeling I could trust her. I wished I could talk to Tabby privately about all of it, but no dice. And with night coming on fast, we didn't even have a place to stay. I was starting to regret agreeing to this trip.

Woody turned her eyes on me. "What are you going to do about it?"

I took a deep breath. No way was I going to lie. Besides, I had the feeling Woody would know if I did anyway. Plus, I had to give her some sort of answer. She had earned that at least for giving us some information. "I've been advised to take a look and report my findings to my superiors."

Woody rocked on her chair. "Lord Jesus. I swear on God's green earth that church can't see. You gonna have to do more than that. You're lucky you got me to help."

I shook my head. This was sounding worse and worse and I hadn't even seen the kid yet. "I can't do anything until I'm told."

Woody sighed and shook her head. "You in trouble already, aren't you?"

I blinked. I had no idea how she knew, but she did. Woody had a lot of hidden talents. "If I step out of line on this…The truth is, I will be in pretty bad shape."

She nodded. Then, she turned to Tabby. "But you, you aren't part of his gobbledygook, are you?"

Tabby swallowed hard. "No, I'm not. But I'm not safe."

"What do you mean?" Woody asked.

Tabby glanced at me. I nodded. She turned back to Woody. "I was possessed by a demon not long ago. I'm still trying to rebuild my protections."

Woody closed her eyes. Without a word, she hopped up and started rummaging through her cupboards. She pulled one thing out, then flung open another cabinet. "It will take a while, but I think I got the thing to help."

"I'm willing to try almost anything."

Tabby seemed more depressed than I had seen her in a while.

Maybe she'd been putting on a mask. The other part of me wondered if Tabby was that desperate or if she felt like she could trust Woody as much as I did. One thing was certain, she and I needed to have a hell of a long talk, and not only about work.

Woody put several bottles of herbs down in front of Tabby. "Make a tea out of these every day. A pinch should be enough. Once you run out, you should be doing better."

"You have no idea how much I appreciate this," Tabby said. She put the bottles in her purse.

Woody patted her on the arm. "I wish I had the time to pass on what I know to you, but we have much more pressing things."

Yeah. Like demon babies. If Woody wasn't so serious about it all, I'd have sworn the woman on the hill was just a weird crack head. She sure looked the part with the broken yellow hair and the wild look in her eyes. Sometimes, I wished for a life mired in normalcy, instead of the paranormal shit storm I bounced around in.

"Jimmy?"

I jerked. "Yeah?"

Tabby sighed. "Any ideas on how you are going to get your proof?"

I stretched and popped my back. "I thought I'd wait until dark, then creep around and try to take a picture of the inside of the house with my phone."

I had given up on the idea of getting to go back home anytime soon. We'd track down a hotel tomorrow. Sleeping in the car for the night wouldn't be all that bad.

Woody laughed. "That's about the dumbest idea I've heard in a while."

Tabby raised her eyebrow at me.

"Okay. You guys got any better ideas?" I asked. Not like I wasn't open to suggestions. I was flying blind here.

Woody lowered herself into a chair. "Sure do. We splash holy water on that woman's feet when she isn't paying attention. I bet anything that devil child is close at her heels."

"It's kind of mean, but I like it," Tabby said.

"I'm so confused." I had no idea what water on that woman's feet would have to do with anything.

Tabby grabbed hold of my head and forced me to look at her. "The plan is to splash the baby with the hold water, doofus. If it screams, you have your proof. If it doesn't, well, unfortunately, from what Woody said, it's gonna scream."

I sighed and took her hands away from my face. She could have explained it a bit nicer than that. But I guess she was annoyed. Whatever. I turned to Woody. "Got any rose petals?"

FOUR
DO OR DIE

AFTER I HAD MADE a batch of my bastardized holy water, I assessed my work. I wanted to quit right then. Somehow, water full of vodka and rose petals with a few words said over it didn't hold the magic it used to for me. It didn't help that it was in a regular plastic bottle. I had no need of the Catholic holy water bottles anymore. But maybe I would need to reassess that idea. Part of the magic was the ritual. If I didn't believe, where did that leave us? And what did it matter to me if that kid was part devil or not? Truly? "This isn't going to work."

Tabby grumbled. "Why not?"

"Because I have to see it. Listening to the little bugger scream isn't going to be enough." I knew better than to release something like that in a report. We could still use the holy water, but we needed something better. Or rather, I needed a hell of a lot more.

"For who?" Woody asked.

"The Order. My bosses." I knew Martin wasn't going to accept just anything. Especially since this was supposed to be for the Church. Part of me wasn't so sure it was as big a deal as they were making it out to be, but then, I had no idea what a devil baby was capable of doing. They should have waited for the experts. There was no hurry here.

Woody grumbled.

I thought for a minute. If I could convince the mother I wasn't a threat somehow, that I didn't mean her child harm, maybe, I could get my eyes on it. That was all I needed. It sure didn't sound that hard. "Hey Tabby."

"Yes?"

"Didn't we see some kid crawl up a wall on one of those home video shows?" It was only a couple of weeks ago—on national TV no less.

"Yeah. Lucy said something about it not being normal, if memory serves." She glanced over at Lucy, who was playing with Doc, and then stared back toward me.

I hopped up from the chair. "I'll be back."

Woody and Tabby gaped at me like I'd swallowed a squirrel.

Maybe I was a bit erratic, but if I didn't follow my impulses, we would get nowhere. I ran to the car, grabbed my phone from the center console, and hurried back into the house.

I sat in the chair in Woody's kitchen and loaded my YouTube app. In a few minutes, I had several videos of "spider children". Not quite how I planned for it to go, but if it worked, what did it matter? Finally, something flashed in my brain. "Now, this might work."

"Do I want to know?" Woody asked.

Tabby sighed. "No, you probably don't."

I grinned. If I could keep this up, I would be able to charm them all. Heh. Even I had to laugh at that. "Only doing what I do best."

That's how I ended up walking up that hill by myself carrying only my cell phone and the vial of holy water in my pocket. It was late afternoon. The heat of the day was baking. I started sweating just from walking up the hill. It was that humid. I felt like a jackass. Maybe I needed to think things through instead of following my impulses. Shit, I didn't know what to do anymore. Seemed like every time I tried something, I did the wrong thing. I needed a vacation from all my problems.

Before I even got ten feet from the porch of the house, the woman ran out the door holding a shotgun. She looked like a crazed backroads inbred woman in a sackcloth dress—something out of an old cowboy movie. Her hair was pulled back from her face but had slipped from the band that was holding it, so she had straggles everywhere. If she hadn't been holding the gun, I might have been amused.

"That's far enough," she said as she cocked the hammer on the gun.

I held up my hands in the universal gesture of "please, don't shoot me". I had no intentions of getting shot. Not today and hopefully not ever. "I mean no harm. I might even be able to help."

A wad of yellowed phlegm landed in the gravel in front of my feet. I never knew someone could supernaturally spit, but I guess there was a first for everything.

I forced myself not to lash out. "Look. Isn't it better to see if I can help? Things can't get much worse can they?"

The woman fired the gun into the air.

I didn't need any other sign. "Fine. I'm going. Don't shoot me in the back."

I turned around and headed down the hill to Woody's. What a mess. This wasn't rocket science. I needed to see her kid—not even take a picture. Granted, a picture would be better, but I was trying for the easiest thing. I could testify to the Order what I saw. Now, however, I was going to have the pleasure of calling the Order and telling them I had failed. It was a first and it sucked. Big time.

As soon as I walked into Woody's house, Tabby's face fell. "What the hell happened?"

I threw myself into the empty chair at the table. Lucy and Doc sat on the floor. Lucy was playing with what I assumed was Woody's spoon. Doc watched her like a grandpa. I focused on Tabby. "I got a gun pulled on me."

"What?" She jumped from her chair and rushed over to me.

I nodded. "12-gauge shotgun."

Her mouth opened and closed a few times, then she hugged me. After a minute, she let me go and stepped back. "Fuck. What are you going to do now?"

I rubbed the back of my neck. "No choice. Gotta call the Order."

Woody walked in from some other part of the house. "Guess you better make a phone call."

Again, here she was seeming to know more about me than she was letting on. It made me a bit uneasy. "Yep."

"Go into the living room for some privacy," she said. "Then come back and we'll figure out what to do."

"Yes, ma'am." I almost saluted her. Thank God I didn't. I would have seemed like a complete idiot.

The living room was as clean as the kitchen. A sofa and chair in a matching light blue color created a warm harmony. A couple of wooden end tables and a lamp on the table between the chair and the sofa completed the picture. There was no TV, just a big fireplace, a picture window that pointed toward the house up above, and a raft of dried herbs and candles. The floor continued with hardwood. You could wear a pair of white gloves and wipe any surface and never find a speck of dust in the place. Made me feel like my scuzzy ass didn't belong.

I installed myself on the sofa and fetched my cell phone from my pocket. This was going to suck. Felt almost as bad as being called into the boss's office when you knew you were about to be fired.

After a few moments, he answered. "Hello?"

"Father Martin?"

"Yes?" I could hear rustling in the background, like he was flipping through something on his desk.

"I have some bad news. The child's mother will not let me see him." I waited for the response, hoping I wasn't going to get yelled at.

Father Martin cleared his throat. "How did she stop you?"

I laughed. "She pointed a shotgun at my face."

I could have described it all in some dramatic fashion, and I suppose in a way I did, but I could have gone over the top—not that it was necessary.

He got all silent. Then, after a minute, I heard him take a breath. "So, it is unsafe."

"That's my take on it. Not supernaturally either." I rubbed my arms. I still had goosebumps. Kind of funny, I didn't get them staring at demons, but I did when someone was going to shoot me. I was weird.

"I can't very well ask our guests to come in on this," Martin said.

But there was something about the way he said it that seemed off. My senses pinged. Here it was. The exact damn thing I was afraid of the whole time. I was sure of it now. "There weren't any guests, were there?"

Father Martin cleared his throat again, but did not say a word. That wasn't a good sign.

"When were you going to tell me?" I asked.

"When it became important." He coughed, and I heard more rustling.

My blood boiled, and I fought not to crush my phone in my hand. "I'm an exorcist, not a fucking babysitter."

"No, you are a Marker. And you are a member of this Order and under contract. I have already gone to bat for you several times. If you wish to keep your employment, you will abide by my wishes. And that child, whether you like it or not, has a soul."

I wasn't about to be pushed around. I didn't care who he was. "If it is like you say it is, it sure as hell ain't human."

He chuckled. "That part doesn't truly matter. You've done it before."

It was my turn to be quiet. I had never told them about what happened to Tabby. Never told them about getting that demon out and killing it with the mark. I had simply said in my report that I had sent the demon inhabiting the dead body back to Hell. No specifics. To be honest, I was surprised they accepted it. But that was beside the point. "Let me guess, if I don't do this, the money stops."

"That is correct." He said it so smugly that if he were standing in front of him, I would have punched him right straight in the mouth.

"Fuck me."

"No, Mr. Holiday. We are blessed that your talent is more than most."

"What the hell is that supposed to mean?" I wished I could reach through that invisible connection and choke the life out of him.

"Mark the child, Mr. Holiday. Then we'll talk." He hung up.

Here I thought it couldn't get worse. "Is this where I get to say, fuck my life?"

I took another minute to steel my nerves. I had to wonder how much was a lie now. Did I not get an interpreter in Italy because the sabotage was meant to happen by the Order? Was Father Martin in on it all? I was so screwed. Part of me wanted to sit outside with Isaac and say to hell with it all.

I got off the sofa and headed back to the kitchen.

Woody wrapped her arm around my shoulders as soon as I entered. "Sit down here, child. One of Woody's cookies will get you right as rain."

She guided me to the chair next to Tabby and turned away from me. Before I knew it, she had placed one the biggest sugar cookies I had ever seen on a plate in front of me. It was about an inch thick and about four inches in diameter. I swear I almost needed a fork. I broke off a piece and shoved it into my mouth. "Oh. My. God."

It melted as soon as it hit my tongue. It was buttery and sweet and light as a feather. I'd never had a cookie like it. I beamed at Woody.

She was grinning from ear to ear. "Now, tell us all about it."

I wasn't sure what to do. I could quit and go home. But that meant having to pinch shit with the chickens. I knew I had nothing to replace this job. It wasn't like I had any other prospects. Still, Tabby could go back and finish her Ph. D. I was kidding no one. It would make me feel awful if she had to go back, and I would have to try to scrape enough of my old contacts together in the hopes of finding a job.

None of it mattered anyway. I couldn't go back to working in an office. I enjoyed doing what I did, albeit the danger and supernatural nonsense. And I had to give Tabby, Woody, Doc, and Lucy credit for listening to me ramble on in between bites of cookie. I needed to buck up. And at the end of it, Tabby told me it was up to me. Ultimately, she was right. The question was, could I live with my answer?

And the kicker? I wasn't exactly sure why we all trusted Woody so much. She was nice, sure. And she'd lived by this crazy woman up the hill who knew how long, but we weren't ourselves.

"You know, you could always sneak in there," Lucy blurted out.

I stared at her for a minute. "What do you mean?"

"Doc can move stuff, right?" Her little face seemed so hopeful.

I checked in with Doc. He shrugged.

She threw her arms up. "Why couldn't he open a window into the house or something?"

Tabby tapped her pointer finger against her chin. "That isn't a bad idea, unless the house is warded."

Woody grunted. "There's no sneaking up on a bad witch—not a living person anyway. Never tried it with a spirit. Could be dangerous though."

"Dangerous how?" Tabby asked.

Woody propped her foot up on her knee. "If she's a necromancer, she could do a spell to take possession of the spirit that enters her house and have it do her bidding."

Doc cleared his throat. "It best be me that goes—"

"No," Lucy said suddenly. She got that sad look I recognized from Italy.

I searched her face, trying to make sure she was okay. I wasn't certain anymore. Most of the happiness she was putting on was most likely an act, but I had no idea what to do about it.

"I knew about Mr. Black when Asmodeus possessed me," she said. "Mr. Black only did the bad magic. I bet I could figure out what she's doing by the magic she does."

I didn't like it. Didn't like it one bit. But as much as I didn't want to admit it, Lucy had a point. She'd seen bad magic before. Probably saw some performed. I didn't have that advantage. And I honestly didn't know what Doc did or didn't know about magic. But Lucy's knowledge was a sure thing.

"All right, how do we get you near the house?" I asked.

"Don't worry, Lucy," Tabby said. "We can be one hell of a distraction."

Lucy smiled.

FIVE

UP IN THE AIR

I ENDED up plodding back up the hill, carrying a sack with some of Woody's cookies and some other food. It took a lot for me to risk getting shot again, but since Lucy was willing to put her ass on the line, it was the least I could do. Besides, it was cookies. Who didn't like cookies?

Before I even got close to the porch, I called, "I come bearing gifts."

Yes, I was being an idiot, but maybe if I kept the tone light, she wouldn't try to kill me. It was worth the attempt.

The woman came out on the porch, holding her gun, but she didn't raise it. That was an improvement. "What kind of gifts?"

"Food. Some cookies for the baby and a few other things." I held the bag open so she could sort of see inside, though I had my doubts as to how much she could make out from that distance. I was trying, dammit.

"What? What's in 'em?"

Who cares? They were cookies. Jesus. "No tricks. I swear. It's only food."

"I still ain't asking you in."

I closed up the bag of food. "That's fine. I wasn't expecting that. Eventually, I'd like to meet with you and your child. But for now, please, this is a gift. Nothing more."

"No strings?" She waddled back and forth.

"Not a one."

She climbed off the porch and snatched the bag from my hand so fast I didn't even see it. I was dealing with a viper instead of a human being.

Then, she pointed her gun at me. "Now, get on out of here. I know where you are if I need your help."

I didn't wait around. I didn't want to be fired at again. That was an experience I'd rather not repeat. I hoped Woody hadn't slipped something in that bag. But who knew what was right at this point? Besides, if I did confirm it was a devil baby, what was I going to do about it? The last demonic thing I marked had died or disappeared into nothingness. Not sure what would happen here since this soul had been born into subhuman flesh.

I needed a drink.

"Is Lucy back yet?" I asked as I walked into the house. They were still seated around the table. Minus Lucy, of course.

"No, she's not," Tabby said.

I exhaled slowly. I had thought she was going to go in, then come right back out again. This didn't bode well. "I hope she's okay."

"If she don't come back in a bit, I'll go after her," Doc said. He hunched over the table with his hat resting behind him on the counter.

"We all will." I took a seat at the table and steeled for a fight.

"Nope," Tabby said. "Let's be logical. Doc is good at staying out of trouble. He can make sure not to get too close to get caught in any type of trap and should still be able to check what's going on with Lucy."

I wiped my hands over my face. This whole thing was a shit storm. "I swear, I don't know which end is up anymore."

Woody laughed. "You should be used to that by now, working for them people. They didn't strike me as anything special when I met them before."

"What?" I twitched

"When I was a little girl."

SIX

WOODY'S STORY

"THINGS WEREN'T LIKE they are now," she began. "Sure, seasons changed, but the differences had to do with crops and harvest. Death and birth. And having been a slave, it was true, life was hard."

I didn't speak. I did the math in my head. In order for Woody to have been a slave, she had to be over one hundred and fifty years old. My body stilled. Woody wasn't normal. Not at all. And she definitely wasn't what I thought she was—a nice old lady. There was much more to her. The question was, exactly how supernatural was she?

"By the time I was sixteen, the war was over. I made my way further north, hoping for a better life. But sadly, people here were every bit as nasty. Work was hard to come by. I took anything I could get. Things got a bit easier when I met Carl. Carl Woods. He was a coal miner. Miners didn't care what color you were. They wanted bodies. Didn't care where they came from. We settled in the coal camp. We had a company house and Carl was paid with scrip."

"What's that?" Tabby asked.

"Company money. It wasn't 'til later they passed laws after a whole bunch of people died. But back then, all the mining families lived and breathed on the company's whim. If they thought coal production wasn't good enough, the store would be closed and we'd go hungry until they punished us enough." She took a sip of her coffee.

Her history broke my heart. Another example of how shitty people could be to each other.

"Lots of types of people in them coal camps. People from all over. Wasn't nothing to hear English, Italian, Polish, and any other Easter European language you could think of on the same street. Everybody tried to survive." She nodded at Tabby. "Not too different from now."

She took a deep breath and exhaled. "One day, a new woman moved onto the next street over. Rumor was she was the boss's mistress, but I never saw no proof of that. She had this stringy blond hair and eyes blue like the ocean. She might have been pretty if she kept herself cleaner. But she didn't seem to like water too much, if you get my drift."

I nodded, not sure where she was going, but it was one hell of a story.

"Anyway," she said. "A few months later, we stopped seeing her around town. It wasn't like she had anyone to help her in that house, but no one would ever go in and no one would ever go out. Word got around that she was with child."

"Did she ever act weird around town?" I asked. "When she went I mean."

"Not sure if you'd classify it as weird per se, but she never went to church. Back then, everybody went to church, whether they liked it or not. Or rather, unless you weren't falling down drunk, you went to church. She never set foot in the building."

I nodded. I wasn't sure if the woman in this story was possessed or simply weird, but I was making mental notes.

"But back to her not being seen at all around town—that in itself wasn't so odd. Yet the rumblings of seeing candles lit in the house late at night and her moving to some beat no one ever heard was plain bizarre. No one danced like that back then.

Heck, most couldn't even afford a radio. And she had no radio. She danced to some beat in her head."

Tabby strummed her fingers on the table. "Could she have been autistic?"

Woody shook her head. "There wasn't anything medically wrong with her. She didn't have tics or avoid eye contact. She was just mean as a snake and didn't do the same things everyone else did. Wasn't long before people started saying she was a witch. Of course, at that time, anyone that did anything they considered weird had to be a witch, but when you walked by her place, you felt something. My mama had taught me a lot about witches when I was a girl. Taught me the old ways, but I never used them—not unless I needed to cure a sickness the doctor wouldn't help with. So I knew what to look for. She was the real thing."

Doc nodded. "Seen a few myself." He jerked his chin toward Tabby. "Besides her I mean."

I chuckled. Tabby threw her napkin at him. Woody rolled her eyes.

"Anyway, I didn't want to cause any trouble for anyone, so I kept my mouth shut. Too many times, I'd seen people accused of things they never did or said. I needed more proof than the word of a few yahoos around town. That and a bad feeling when I walked by her house. For all I knew, what I was feeling could have to do with what was buried underneath her house." She glanced at me. "I was stupid for not trusting my instincts."

She rubbed her hands over her arms as if brushing away a chill. "Finally, one day, the boss asked my friend Mary if she'd help with the birth. Mary didn't want to, but she was stuck. If she didn't do what the boss wanted, her husband would lose his job, get hurt, or wind up dead. It was a risk she couldn't afford to take."

"I've heard about the special scrip before," I said quietly.

Woody blinked. "The Esau scrip you mean?"

I nodded.

"What are you talking about?" Tabby asked.

"The owners of the coal company would issue Esau scrip—essentially a paper loan that helped the women's families get by when work was scarce or their husbands were sick. Basically, it meant they sold themselves to the men in power. Sometimes it was even forced. That's why so many women and kids went without shoes. They traded new shoes for sex."

Tabby put her hand over her mouth. "Oh my God. That's awful."

Woody nodded. "Of course, the night of the birth came faster than any of us thought. Mary was in there for hours. I helped by bringing her warm buckets of water so things would be ready when the time came. No one else offered to help."

Her eyes seemed to drift away back to a time when none of us were born. "Suddenly, I heard a scream. Mary ran out of that house, down the steps, and away. I lost sight of her. When I turned around, through the window, I spied it. The baby had horns and a tail—and it was halfway to the ceiling, climbing up the walls—umbilical cord still attached. Blood smeared all over the wallpaper and dripped onto the floor. It whipped its head around and hissed at me."

"Jesus," I said.

"That ain't all of it," Woody said. "Next day, bunch of priests took her and that baby to Pittsburgh, never to be seen again. There weren't even any rumors—nobody knew anything after that."

"And that lady up there is like that one?" I asked.

Woody shrugged. "Ain't seen it, so I don't know. What I can tell you is that the woman on the hill looks awfully familiar, and I'm a lot older than I look."

SEVEN

SAVIOR

WOODY LEFT to go to the bathroom, or so she said. I wasn't sure of anything anymore. My head spun.

"What are we going to do?" Tabby asked. She fidgeted in her seat.

I stared up at the ceiling, then down at Tabby. "I think I better go do something I haven't done in a very long time."

"What's that?"

"Pray."

I went back out onto the porch and glanced up at the sky. Knowing the Order was a lie, or at least my involvement with it, hurt more than I imagined. I'd trusted them. Their whole sense of false brotherhood and the knowledge that something as sacred as this power had been corrupted by man was almost too much to take. I'd lived my whole life waiting for the other shoe to drop, and now it had.

Yet, a real devil baby wasn't anything to mess with, and the fact that Lucy was trapped up there or something meant I needed to get my ass in gear. I hadn't protected her this long to let her be controlled by a witch—if that was what was going on. And knowing what Lucy could do, well, it didn't sit with me that she could be used as a weapon. She wasn't to be used at all. She was still a little girl, no matter how she acted.

Isaac meowed. I bent down and petted him through the door of the carrier. It was cooler here on Woody's porch. Almost as if she had spelled the place. What was I thinking? She probably had.

"God. What do I do? I'm lost here."

I stared into the yard. The sun shone on Woody's flowers, a myriad of colors. It was beautiful, but it told me nothing. Of course, I couldn't be all that mad at the man upstairs. It wasn't like I took the time to talk to him. When was the last time someone had asked him how his day was going? It sure as hell hadn't been me. I needed to do better.

"Boy."

I searched the yard.

"Boy?"

I whipped my head in the direction of the voice. The old man, Charlie, stood there. He spit a jaw of tobacco juice on the ground. "You done lollygaggin'?"

"I guess so."

He grunted. "Better get a move on. Looks like storm's coming."

I checked the sky. No cloud in sight. By the time I turned my head to look at him, he was gone.

"I'll be a sonofabitch."

Charlie was a ghost or something. Woody never said. But I had asked God for an answer, so I took Charlie at his word.

"So?" Tabby asked when I entered the kitchen.

"We're fucked." And the bad part was, I was serious. All of this was riding on my shoulders and I was known for not being steady. This needed someone with a hell of a better handle on all this than me, but I guess God knew what he was doing. Still, it didn't help me not to be scared about it.

"How bad?" Doc asked.

I shrugged. "No sign of Lucy anywhere."

Tabby seemed to quiver. "Should we send in Doc?"

I sighed. "And get another one lost? I don't think so."

Doc grunted at me and disappeared.

"Great. Just great."

"Now, what do we do?" Tabby asked.

I wished I had something to throw, but I had nothing. Not anything that was mine that I could afford to break anyway.

Tabby danced from foot to foot. I'd never seen her this nervous. "Now we have two of them to get back. If too much more happens, I am going to need a psychiatrist."

"Good luck with that, honey. No one will believe either one of us." I walked over and pulled her into a hug.

"How do we fight them?"

"With me," Woody said. She had changed into a colorful caftan with a set of beads wrapped around her hand. The beads were the color of turquoise, but more like the milky translucence of rose quartz. I'd never seen anything like it. In her other hand she held what looked like a chicken's foot.

Tabby took two steps back. "Don't let it touch you, Jimmy."

Woody laughed. "The girl child is right. Any touch of the claw and badness will befall."

I stepped back. Not that I knew what a dried up old chicken foot would do, but Tabby sure as hell seemed scared of it. "How will that get Lucy back?"

Woody grinned. "I'm hoping the threat of it will. If not, we have some problems on our hands."

Twilight danced on the horizon as we three hiked up the hill. We still had a couple hours of daylight. Thank God this was the time of year when it didn't get dark until around eight or so. I had to get my spirit back, take care of the devil baby, get us all home safe and sound, and plan a wedding. It was impossible.

Before we even got near the house, Doc popped in front of us. "Don't go no further."

I froze. "What are you talking about? We need to get Lucy and go home."

Doc shook his head. "Lucy doesn't want to come with you no more."

I noticed then that Doc didn't quite sound like himself. His language was off. In fact, he didn't look quite right. Kind of oddly washed out. I smelled a rat.

"Where is Doc?" I asked.

And the phantom disappeared. "Dammit."

"That witch got more tricks than the feathers on a turkey," Woody said.

"So, what do we do now?" Tabby asked.

"We keep going up the hill, waiting for the next booby trap to pop up." Woody started plodding forward. Tabby and I followed.

"Where are they, you think?" I asked Woody.

"Might be in ghost boxes. Might be something else."

"What's a ghost box?" Tabby asked.

"The Jews call them dybbuk boxes, but every culture has them. Since we don't know for sure, don't be looking for one."

I knew what a dybbuk box was, thanks to Lucy and her obsession with exorcism movies. A dybbuk box was used to capture a spirit. If you opened it, the spirit would be let loose. My life was starting to seem like a movie. At this rate, I wasn't going to live to old age.

At the top of the hill, we paused at the driveway.

Woody spun around and stared at me. "You ready for this?"

I nodded.

"Good." She stepped onto the driveway. The air around me grew heavier.

"Get back!" Woody yelled.

A gun shot sounded, and gravel flew in multiple directions at my feet. "Fuck!"

I glared at the woman on the porch holding the gun.

"Give me back what is mine," I said. This was enough. I was tired of her shooting at me. She was going to have to just do it. I didn't care anymore.

She laughed. "Trespassing makes anything on my land mine."

Bullshit. If that's all it took, then we'd all be running around yelling *finders keepers*. "Uh. Uh. The land belongs to the dead. We're the trespassers."

Woody laughed. "You know more than you let on, boy."

I glanced over at her. "I keep stuff close to my chest."

"Let her go," Tabby said.

The witch snarled. "They will come home when they want to."

Tabby stood ram-rod straight with her hands down at her sides. "No, you let them go now. You don't even know what you have."

The evil one smiled. "And what do you think you have?"

"Hell," Tabby said without blinking.

The woman grunted. "You can have them when I'm done with them."

I'd had about enough of this. They weren't hers. They weren't mine. If Lucy and Doc belonged to anyone, it was God. "Look. We've been nice up 'til now. Either you give them back, or I'll take your son. It's as easy as that."

She pointed her gun at me. "No one's taking my boy."

I wasn't scared anymore. This woman could bite me. "Then give them back."

Woody stepped in front of me and held up that chicken's foot. The witch dropped her gun and backed up. "I didn't know you knew that."

"I know a lot more than you think," Woody said. "Now, give them back."

The bad witch swallowed. "I'll set them free. What they choose to do after that, well, that's out of my control."

"Fair enough."

The woman went back inside her house. Various lights turned on and off. I felt a tap on my shoulder. I spun and very faintly, I could see Doc. The real one this time.

"We need to get out of here," he said.

I motioned to the others. "Come on. Let's get safe."

With no argument from the peanut gallery, we all headed down the hill to Woody's. All the while I kept my eyes open for signs of Lucy, but none came.

We sat around Woody's living room. Tabby and I took up the sofa while Woody and Doc rested in armchairs. Doc had a pensive look on his face, but that wasn't what disturbed me. What scared me was the fear in his eyes. Doc never got afraid.

"We got bad trouble," he said.

Tabby took a sip of her coffee. "How bad?"

"Lucy ain't herself no more."

"What do you mean?" I set my cup on the end table and stared at him.

"That woman did something to her. Played on those things we talked about before." He scratched his chin.

When we'd been in Italy, Lucy had started doing things that hurt others. Partly as a result of being incapable of being a regular little girl again. But we'd made her happy—at least I thought we had. I must have been wrong.

"She's not coming back?" Tabby asked.

Doc shrugged. "Dunno. Even if she does, she ain't right. More like them things you fight instead of a kid."

Dammit. I knew from experience that ghosts could join the realm of the demonic. But I thought my mark protected her from it. I didn't know enough and no way but personal experience to learn it all. Would have been nice to have been given a little booklet. But no, I got half-assed training at an exorcism school I couldn't understand. Got kicked out and had a mentor who had an agenda and wanted to use me.

"Are you sure it isn't a spell over Lucy?" Tabby asked.

Doc paused. "Could be. I didn't see it if that's what it was. Of course, I wasn't allowed to see much."

I curled my fingers into a fist. "Did you get to see it at least?"

"It?" His brows scrunched.

"The baby."

Doc laughed. "Oh yeah, I saw *it* all right."

"And?" Jesus. It was like waiting for someone to tell you if you got approved for a mortgage.

"Better get your holy water ready, bucko."

"What happened?" Tabby asked.

Doc sighed. "I was trying to save you the awful details, but guess sometimes it's your right to know."

EIGHT

DOC'S STORY

"I WENT UP THERE. Couldn't hear nothing from outside the house, so I went on in like usual."

I assumed he meant through the wall, but I didn't ask. I didn't want to mess up his story. And besides, it didn't matter how he got in anyway.

"Once I was inside, I could hear again. She must have the house spelled not to let out the sound, if you know what I mean." After scratching his chin, he stared at me. "Anyway, I was there trying not to be noticed, and she comes over carrying what looked to me like a human leg bone. Humerus to be exact. And suddenly, I couldn't move. I couldn't speak. And most importantly, I couldn't dematerialize."

"What type of spell would that be?" Tabby asked.

"Very black magic," Woody said. "The type you only get messing with the dead."

Doc nodded. His form seemed to flit in and out a bit, like there was something off with the feed. Could have been his emotional state, but I had no idea.

"Body parts littered the floor," he said. His lips curled and he paused and wiped his forehead. "Most were animals: cats, dogs, rodents, deer, but there was some human too. The little bundle of joy liked to chew on them."

"Chew?" I almost gagged. The thought of the amount of bacteria laying around all that had me twitching, not to mention the body parts.

Doc rubbed his hands together. "The little dickens has bumps on his scalp like the buds of horns, claws on his hands and feet, and fangs."

"You shitting me?" I asked.

"Nope. Ain't never seen nothing like it."

I scrubbed a hand down my face. "I guess we have to admit it. We have a real devil baby after all."

"As far as I could see," Doc said.

"Your sight, I trust. Now, what the hell do we do about it?"

Doc shrugged. "I think that's for you to decide."

"And the Order expects you to take care of it?" Tabby asked.

"That's what they said." More and more, I was starting to see how far astray I'd been led. I didn't like it. And what made it worse was that Tabby had been trying to tell me for a while to watch my back. I should have listened to her.

"So call the real guys," Woody replied.

"Who?" I asked.

Woody smiled. "The Vatican."

NINE

FALLEN

ONE DIDN'T SIMPLY CALL up the Vatican. When I'd been a priest, anything we couldn't handle was reported to our direct superior. I had never in my life talked to anyone at the Vatican directly. And of course, I knew no Italian. That left me with one hell of a road block.

With no better ideas, I decided to call the Catholic Church at home, St. Mary's. I could only hope someone would be there to answer. It was after business hours. What's the worst that could happen? I could always leave a message. Didn't look like we were going anywhere anytime soon.

"St. Mary's. How may I direct your call?" the secretary asked when she answered the phone.

I almost dropped it. I hadn't expected someone to pick up. "I'd like to talk to the priest, please."

"And who may I say is calling?"

"Jimmy Holiday." To be honest, it was kind of nice not to have someone sneer at me the minute I said my name. When I got back home, maybe I'd visit the church.

"One moment."

The line was dead while I waited. I was thankful for no

cheesy elevator music. These days, I was thankful for the small things.

"Mr. Holiday?"

"Yes."

"I'm Father Montgomery. How can I help you?"

I wasn't sure if I should start with niceties or get to business right away. But there was no easy way to talk about a devil baby. "This is going to sound so strange. Heck, maybe I shouldn't even explain the whole thing and ask for the phone number of your superior."

Father Montgomery cleared his throat. "Mr. Holiday. That isn't something I give out very often. And considering I don't even know you…"

"Point taken. Okay. What do you know about exorcism?" I could almost hear the groan. It was not easy to get anywhere this way. Father Montgomery sighed. "Not much beyond what you see in movies."

"I kind of figured that. Truth is, I'm an exorcist, and I've run into an interesting problem. I need to talk to whoever it is in the Vatican that takes care of interesting problems."

"I have to say you have made my day, Mr. Holiday. Are you a rogue exorcist or something?"

I laughed. If it were that damn simple. Not one thing about my life was easy anymore and it hadn't been for a very long time. "Nothing that entertaining. I'm a member of the Order of Markers."

"I have no idea what that is."

Great. I wanted to punch someone. "Tell you what. Take down my number and call your superior and see if he's heard of the Order. Then give me a call back."

Father Montgomery faintly grumbled. "All right. I'll call back soon."

After he hung up, I started pacing. I didn't blame him for being annoyed. My call had put a heck of a monkey wrench into his routine. It was probably stupid, but I didn't know what else to do.

"Is everything okay?" Tabby asked from the other room.

Great. I sat down. No reason to worry anyone yet. Or at least worry them more than I already had. "Yeah, waiting for a call back."

"Let us know if you need anything." I could hear them moving every so often, but mostly they were quiet.

"Will do."

After about twenty minutes, the phone rang again. I hesitated to answer it, mostly out of fear. But I swallowed my pride and swiped the screen.

"Hello?"

"Mr. Holiday?"

"Father Montgomery, hello." At least he didn't sound quite so annoyed. That was a plus.

"Kicked out of the Vatican's exorcism school, eh?"

My strength fell out of my asshole and rolled across the floor. Fuckers. I kept my cool though. No sense in making things worse. "They know about that, huh?"

Father Montgomery laughed. "The file I'm looking at is pretty darn funny."

It wasn't a dickheaded laugh though. Kind of good natured. I calmed down. "I can only imagine."

I heard some rustling of papers on his end. "What is it you've found?"

"A devil baby."

The good father choked.

"Yeah, I know how it sounds." I did have a tendency to spring things on people. But I felt like it was similar to ripping off a band aid. Better to get the shock over with so we could get on with it.

"I don't envy you, you know?"

I chuckled. "I don't think anyone does."

He took a deep breath. "My superior, Bishop Edwards, has

given me permission to give you his number. I wish I could see his face when he gets your call."

"I'm sure it's going to be a heck of a surprise."

After he gave me the number, I got off the phone and went into the kitchen. I'd made it to the first rung on the ladder at least.

"So?" Doc said.

"Bureaucracy at its finest. I have a phone number for a bishop." I set my phone on the table and sat.

"You get to do this all over again?" Tabby asked.

"Looks that way." It did suck, but it was part of the whole process. The church kept track of everything. And most importantly, they wanted to see if your story changed.

"This is taking too long," Tabby said.

The church wasn't known for its speediness. "That's the church. Got any better ideas?"

Tabby shrugged. "We could try to summon Lucy."

Woody even stared wide-eyed at Tabby.

"Do you think it would work?" I couldn't believe I was even discussing it. But we needed some of this stuff fast. It was another option and it wouldn't hurt to see if something else was better.

Tabby shrugged. "We are so beyond the rules at this point, I don't think it would hurt to try."

She was right. I wasn't sure what path I was following anymore. "And to think it used to be me who came up with the whacked out ideas."

She hit me on the arm.

"Ow!"

Woody sighed. "If we are doing a summoning, we best move to the working room."

"I'll stay right here if you don't mind," Doc said. His eyes kept shifting back and forth and his right hand hovered near his hip, almost as if he was ready to grab for his gun.

I didn't blame him. The fact that he'd been trapped wasn't

cool. He'd managed to survive death for this long, no sense in making it easier for the forces that wanted him out of this world. "No problem. Hopefully, if stuff works out right, we'll be bringing her to you."

Doc grunted.

I followed Woody down a hallway to the back of her house. Tabby trailed behind me. On one side was Woody's bedroom. Her bed had a curly oak frame with a handmade quilt on top. On the other side, the door was closed.

"Don't touch anything unless I tell you. Some things in here are better left alone." Woody opened the door.

The room was dark. The walls were paneled in some deep stained wood. Shelves and shelves of herbs, stones, and jars of things I wasn't sure I wanted to know about lined the walls. Viney things strung together with garlic and old bulby type supplies. I was in another world.

The floor was made of slate—the type used for old fashioned chalk boards. I was almost afraid to walk on it, but it felt sturdy underneath. No give at all. Tabby and I stood in the middle and waited. Woody came in and closed the door behind her.

"I never would have thought to use slate," Tabby said, looking all over the floor.

Woody grinned. "They were tearing down an old school not far from here, so I laid claim to several of the chalkboards. Then, I had some men make it into the floor for the room here. Was perfect so I could make sure each casting circle was clean of any residue from the previous casting."

"I'm sure it makes things easier." Tabby beamed. "All you'd need to do is mop the floor."

"Exactly." Woody stared at me for a second.

"All right, how are we doing this?" I asked.

Woody pointed and motioned for me to move near to the wall. "You can sit there. Should be safe enough."

I nodded and sat where she had told me.

Tabby knelt down at Woody's feet. Woody started drawing

on the floor in chalk. Various symbols and a large circle similar to what I'd seen Tabby draw numerous times. Her symbols were slightly different though.

When she was done, she sat on the floor next to Tabby and stared at her. "All right, child. Your turn."

I watched Tabby take a long, deep breath. Then, from her pocket, she pulled out a folded piece of paper, unfolded it, and placed it in the middle of the circle. I recognized it as a page from one of Lucy's coloring books. Tabby sure as hell was more resourceful than me.

"Hail guardians of the watchtowers of the north, south, east, and west. Hear my call. I need your safety and protection from the spell work I am to do this day." She touched the circle and the boundary glowed her usual green.

She closed her eyes. "Lucy Marie Andersen. I call to you. Come to me."

I felt a shiver down my spine. She kept her eyes closed.

"Lucy, please come back to us."

The shiver got stronger and started to burn.

"Lucy—"

"Stop!" I couldn't take it anymore. It was like something was trying to rip me apart every time she spoke. It was wrong. So very wrong. "Fuck!" The pain finally started receding. "I'm the one who marked her. I own her soul until 'they' figure what to do with it. When you summon her, you are summoning me. Shit. I wish I would have figured that out sooner."

Tabby and Woody both stared at me.

The pain in my back didn't subside until I crawled inside the circle. It wasn't smart, but it had hurt that much. My ass dragged the line of the circle with me, but luckily, it didn't break. I could still feel the power. Except it was outside of me instead of keeping me out. Now, I knew why you weren't supposed to summon spirits.

"Jimmy?" Tabby asked.

"Shh."

I readied myself and closed my eyes. "Lucy, honey. Come here. We need to set things right."

A whoosh encompassed the circle, and then standing in front of me in the circle was Lucy. Her eyes glowed red.

I tried to keep my lifeforce calm and steady. I did not need to give her fear to feed on. "I know it hurts. And I know you have a right to be pissed off at me. But that lady isn't good."

"And what do you know about it?" She snarled.

I sighed. "Because right now, you remind me of Asmodeus."

Her form took a step back and shuddered. Her eyes went back to their usual blue.

"Did that lady do that to me?" she asked, her voice quivering.

I shook my head. "I don't know, honey. I wasn't there."

Lucy ran into my arms, sobbing.

I held her. I could feel her energy resting against me. At least the witch hadn't leeched her power. The poor kid had that happen too many times.

"Jimmy!"

I glanced up and jerked away. Lucy's eyes were red and she held a knife above her head.

"No," I said calmly. Part of me flashed back to the possessed Lucy at Sorrow's Point. But that was impossible. A spirit could not be possessed. A demon wanted a body and Lucy had none to give.

She struggled, her body contorting and squirming. Her arm could not bring down the knife, no matter how hard she tried.

My Mark meant something more than her soul was going to God. I had some type of control over her I didn't entirely understand. "Now, I don't know what nonsense she fed you, but you need to realize that I own you. As ugly as that sounds, it's the truth. And that woman up there wants to own you too—except she wants to do more. She wants to use you. And that's what she's doing right now. She wants you to kill me because of her baby. And even worse, that baby in there isn't even human."

I took the knife from her hand. She snarled at me. I ignored it.

"What are you going to do, Jimmy?" Tabby asked.

I sighed and glanced at Woody. "Got a wooden box I can use?"

I didn't want to put Lucy in the box, but I had no choice. I couldn't watch my back all day and night. And I also didn't want her hurt. I gave her a new name and sealed her in the box with some melted wax and ash guided by Woody. It didn't have to be sealed all the way. It was only symbolism. She was barred from being summoned by her new name as well as the old one. A name only I knew because I thought it instead of saying it aloud. That evil witch could only get it if she killed me. And for now, I'd stopped that from happening. Yay, me.

It was honestly pretty damn scary that someone could turn Lucy into this thing. I didn't even know what to call her at this point. She wasn't a little girl anymore. I couldn't even call her my friend. That tended to change when one tries to kill you.

"Guess we better let Doc know what's going on," I said to them.

Tabby swiped at her eyes. "I wish we didn't have to."

Maybe I'd gone cold, but I didn't have the same trepidation as Tabby. "He will understand. Come on. Let's get to it. We still have things to do."

Woody took the box from my hands and set it on the shelf in her spellroom.

TEN
THIS IS WAR

"YOU WEREN'T KIDDING," I said to Doc as we went into the kitchen. I grabbed the back of the chair, wrapping my fingers around the frame and squeezing.

Doc skulked at the table. "You can't say I didn't warn you." I nodded. "I had to contain her."

He swallowed hard. "I was afraid of that."

Woody and Tabby took the other seats at the table. I paused a few moments more to give Doc some meager time to grieve. Then, I sat and interlocked my fingers on the tabletop before asking, "What should we do now?"

"Try to call that bishop man and see where you get. I will try to figure out a back-up plan," Woody said.

"Doc and I will try to figure out something too. None of this seems to be going the way we think it will. So with three plans, we have a better chance." Tabby smiled weakly at Doc.

"Works for me. Maybe us two numbskulls will come up with something," Doc said. He seemed uncomfortable, and me getting away from him for a bit was probably a good thing.

"All right. Wish me luck." I left and went back into the living room. I wasn't looking forward to this phone call. I punched in the number and got one of those strange busy signals. I took the phone from my ear and confirmed I had plugged in the number right. Then, I tried dialing again. Same thing.

"Shit." There was too much wrong about all of this for me not to believe that something supernatural was afoot. Whether it was the witch, or Martin, or whoever the fuck it was, I was not happy.

I tried once more before giving up, then I headed into the kitchen once more. Tabby and Doc were making notes on a piece of paper.

"Done already?" Tabby asked.

"Can't get through. Like something doesn't want me to get any help. Big surprise, eh?" I sat and lounged in the chair until my head touched the back. I closed my eyes.

"Why do I have the feeling we are dealing with more than just the workings of your Order?" Doc asked.

I opened my eyes and stared at him. "That was my thought too, though I feel like even the Order ain't on the up and up anymore."

"What are you going to do?" Tabby asked.

I exhaled. "I don't like the thought of leaving now. That woman did something to Lucy. And whatever it was, isn't good. Either she fixes it, or I'll—"

"Kill it?" Tabby asked before I could finish.

I sat up sharply. "God, no. It needs to go where it belongs. That means that Big Red will likely show up at some point."

"Oh, that sounds like such a fabulous idea. Let's give the Devil what he wants—his one begotten son. Jesus." Tabby threw her hands above her head and rolled her eyes.

I shook my head. "It isn't his only son. Don't forget Vespa. I would say this demon child is the result of copulation between one of Big Red's minions and that witch up there. Not one of Big Red's kids. Besides, can you see him having sex with that?"

Tabby held her head in her hands. "I don't even want to think about it."

The back door opened, and Woody stepped through. "I don't know about you all, but I could use a drink."

"That sounds good," Tabby replied.

"It will be full dark soon."

I peered through the window. She was right, and I didn't feel safe. Something felt heavy about the entire place. So much had happened and I was still trying to wrap my head around the fact that at eight o'clock this morning I was talking to Tabby about going to the wedding planner. Jesus.

Woody walked over and placed her hand on my shoulder. "Let's get us a drink, then we can prepare the house for the night. You better stay here. Safer."

"My cat is outside," Tabby said.

Woody tapped her chin. "Better run and get him."

Doc and I stayed at the table, staring at each other. It felt like the scene in *Jaws* when the fishermen sing while they are all drinking...right before the shark attacks the boat.

Tabby set Isaac's carrier on the floor.

Woody looked down at her. "I'll have to request that you don't let him out. Things aren't safe here for him."

Tabby nodded. "Okay. If you say so."

Woody crossed the kitchen and closed and locked the door to the porch. Tabby sat at the table and waited for instructions. Woody stared out the window. After a moment, she jerked back and pulled the curtain closed.

It was just weird enough to make me uneasy. Woody wasn't the type that was easily scared. "What's wrong?"

"They're already walking. We stay inside tonight." Woody walked over to the counter and put her hands on it as if steeling herself.

"Who's walking?" Tabby asked.

"The dead," Woody answered.

Doc laughed. "Not like me."

Woody turned around and shook her head. "No, not like you

at all. These are the ungrateful dead. This mountain has a history."

"Like what?" I blinked. This was far stranger than even I had imagined and I'd seen a lot of weird at this point.

Woody swallowed. "No time for that now." She loaded up several pitchers of water. "Go around the house. Coat every window sill and doorway to the outside in this house. Make sure it is very wet."

"Why?" None of this made any sense to me.

Her eyes snapped in my direction. "Dammit. I said no questions."

Tabby and I hopped up and started rubbing water everywhere. I glanced at Tabby, and she shrugged. After we'd moved through a room, Woody followed behind and did it again. Finally, she collapsed a living room chair.

"Come and sit down," she waved at us.

Tabby collected the pitchers and took them to the kitchen. I sat on the couch, careful not to get any wetness on it. I watched Doc walk down the hallway and dematerialize into what I assumed was the spellroom.

"Now, to answer your question, Mr. Holiday. Witches can't pass running water." Woody stared at me and waited.

I turned to Tabby.

Woody laughed. "Not her. Bad witches. Running water purifies. A bad witch will burn in running water."

"I thought that was an old story," Tabby said, visibly shivering.

Woody stared off into space. "Lots of these old stories have basis in fact. The trick is to find the reality hidden within."

"What are you?" I asked.

Her eyes came back to the present. "Mambo. A high priestess. I try not to practice so much anymore. Compared to others, I didn't practice much at all. Most of the time, it wasn't safe to do so. A lot of the old ways are dark. But sometimes, there is no choice but to fight dark with dark."

"So you can't pass either." I cupped my chin.

"Now, what gave you that idea, silly boy? Just because I know the dark, don't mean I'm evil. Gotta have the right mind for that." She readjusted herself in the chair as if she was in pain.

"It's more than that," I said.

Woody smiled. "You do know, then."

"Unfortunately." Had too much experience with true evil at this point not to know. Living and dead.

Tabby addressed Woody. "I'm not sure if we're on the same side or if you just want something."

Woody chuckled. "If I wanted something, I would have let that thing up there have what she wanted."

Tabby leaned forward. "Pardon me for wondering. Seems lately, every time I trust someone, I get screwed."

"You've been trusting the wrong people."

"Maybe."

I wanted to go home. This whole thing royally sucked. I needed a new life.

"Now that we've had that lovely conversation," Tabby glared at me, "why don't we try to relax so we can make it through the night?"

Doc appeared in front of me. "I can hear them."

I jerked back. I wasn't used to him doing that. He tried to walk through doorways and stuff usually. But today had everyone off kilter.

"Who?" Tabby asked.

"The ones outside," he replied, then glanced over toward the big picture window next to Woody's chair.

Woody nodded.

"What's the story?" I asked.

She gave me a macabre smile, almost as if she was granting me an audience. "At one point, there was a cemetery above the witch's house. Long before the witch lived there. Don't know what type of magic laid waste, but at night, the dead walk."

Something hammered against the kitchen door. I jumped.

"You aren't talking about ghosts, are you?" I asked.

Woody smacked her lips. "In voudou, there are ways to make the dead do what you want."

My mind flipped through a thousand images. Slowly, the realization dawned on me. I felt like bugs were crawling up my legs. "Are we talking about zombies? Please tell me we aren't talking about fucking zombies."

"Reality is worse than fiction, isn't it?" Woody grinned.

Tabby coughed and ran a hand through her hair. "Will the water do anything to them?"

"No. Not a thing. We are safe with the protections."

"What do we do if they make it into the house?" It wasn't like I carried a gun. Otherwise, I'd just shoot them in the head.

"These aren't like the ones from your movies, Mr. Holiday. They do not eat the flesh of humans for sustenance. They don't eat anything at all. They are dead. But they carry nasty bacteria, and when provoked, have been known to kill."

Like that made everything all better. I needed a stiff drink. "Okay, let me get this straight. You live in a home surrounded by zombies at night?"

"Can't think of a better free security system."

Tabby jumped when one of them thumped against the side of the house.

"What if the witch controls them?" I asked.

"Impossible." Woody waved off my question. "Zombies are controlled only by the Houngan or Mambo that creates them. Even if she wants to, she can't control them."

Yeah, this was the stuff of old movies like *White Zombie*. No parasite or chemical bullshit here. Zombies were magic.

"Where is the one who created them?" Doc asked.

Woody chuckled. "Long dead, I expect. He or she never thought they could pass on ownership."

"Wait, there is a horde of wandering zombies outside?" I had this image in my head of rotting corpses dropping body parts at various areas around the house. Maybe that's why Woody's flowers were so beautiful—fertilization.

"Don't trivialize it. I assure you, Mr. Holiday. If you go outside, or one of them becomes agitated by something like that cat in the other room, you won't think this is a big laugh at all."

I felt like a shit. I'd been disrespectful as all hell. And without reason. I needed to keep my head together. "I'm sorry."

Woody grunted. "Your mouth gets you in a lot of trouble."

"You have no idea." Tabby glared at me.

I threw my hands in the air and glanced back and forth between them. "Thanks a lot."

"I think the problem is you don't have your little conscience," Doc said.

I glanced toward Woody's spellroom. "God, I miss her."

"We all do," Tabby said.

"We will fix her, even if I have to do extra research," Woody said.

Minus the lumps and bumps during the night, I slept all right. It was pretty surprising, given all the shit that had happened. Woody holed herself up in her bedroom. I let Tabby have the couch, and I slept in Woody's chair. It seemed like the right thing to do. Doc wandered around and kept an eye on things. If I hadn't been so chicken I would have opened a curtain wide enough to look at one of those zombies. But I didn't. Not much gave me nightmares these days; I wanted to keep it that way. Knowing they were out there was bad enough. As soon as the sky began to brighten, the bumps stopped. I could breathe again. Woody came out of her bedroom and motioned for me to follow her into the kitchen.

I got up from the chair and followed as quietly as I could.

Once I entered the room, Isaac meowed softly at me and I

reached down and gently scratched his head through the bars of the crate. I figured the poor guy needed to use the restroom bad.

"Is it okay to let him out now?" I asked.

Woody nodded. She opened the porch door and I opened his carrier. He shot out like a light. I glanced inside the carrier. He'd been really good. Hadn't made a mess at all. I wished he would have gone though. I didn't want to worry about him getting a bladder infection or something. He didn't need to suffer just because my job made things difficult.

Woody quietly set a bowl of water on the floor, along with a small plate with a bit of tuna on it.

"Change your mind?" I asked her.

She sighed. "I normally don't like animals in the house. Lots of dirt. But he can't stay in that thing forever."

"Tabby will be happy." I smiled.

"I thought so."

As soon as I saw Isaac coming up the steps, I opened the door. He ran over to the water and got a drink. Then, he rubbed against Woody's legs. She glanced down at him, chuckled, and made her way over to the table.

"Are you afraid to die, Mr. Holiday?"

If I had coffee, I would have spat it out. I wasn't sure how to answer her. My life had gotten so much more complicated than that. "I used to say no. Now, I'm not so sure."

Woody nodded. "You have more to lose."

I scratched my arm. "And the thought of not making things right before I die scares the crap out of me."

"You do realize most people don't get what they want before death, right?" She got up and started pulling food from the fridge.

"I'm hoping someone can put in a good word for me up there." The way things were looking, I was going to need it.

Woody laughed. "I can see why she puts up with you."

Doc came in. "With all the lollygagging going on in here,

sounds like you know how to save the world. How do we fix Miss Lucy?"

Woody placed a pan on the stove. "One way is very easy; however, it will not be palatable for those here."

Doc grunted.

"What do you mean?" I asked.

She shrugged. "We could kill her. But like I said, not palatable."

I forced my anger not to show in my voice. For her to even think like that...more and more I wasn't sure if Woody was practical or if there was something else there. Of course, maybe I needed to stop being so sensitive. "In order to fix her, that means we have to get her where we can connect with her." I knew what it was going to take to pull that off, and it required more out of me than what I may have been able to give. But if I were honest, things kept extracting their pound of flesh, and I was getting grumpier as time went on.

"You all talking about me," Tabby said from the doorway.

I laughed. "I wish."

"Pull up a chair and get ready for breakfast," Woody said while tending to some eggs.

Before long, there were mountains of food. Part of me wanted to give her money for the food, but I knew it would insult her. I was tired of walking on eggshells.

"What's the plan?" Tabby asked.

"Looks like I gotta play double naught spy and try to kidnap a baby." Again, not that any of this had been spoken aloud, but I was betting that was the point. Woody wanted me to come up with solutions on my own. Or maybe God did. I was so confused.

"Boy, are we in trouble." Tabby rolled her eyes.

ELEVEN

CLOSER TO THE EDGE

IT WASN'T LIKE I had ever kidnapped anyone before, let alone a witch with a devil baby. I had more to worry about than baby cries. Stuff like jail time, fines, and possibly, some dude named Bubba.

"Now that the witch doesn't have Lucy, seems like as long as we create a hell of a distraction, I can go in there, take said baby and hold it for ransom in exchange for fixing Lucy." I was talking out of my ass. I had no idea what I was doing.

"One big problem, bucko," Doc said. "Last time I checked, it was still illegal to kidnap a baby."

That made me pull up my boot straps real quick. In everything I'd done against the demonic, I'd kept free of any legal wrongdoing. If I did something bad, that put me at a serious disadvantage and was not something I wanted to explore. I was ill-prepared enough. "Okay, next plan?"

"Why not befriend the child. Make it feel safe so that when you call to it, the child will come," Woody suggested.

"And then what?" I wanted to know where she was going with this.

"If you don't leave the grounds, you are not kidnapping the

child. And if the child is held without distress, you are doing nothing wrong."

"What if the witch tricks us again?" I asked.

"We put a spell on her that prevents her from lying or causing us any harm," Tabby said.

It was starting to sound like something that made sense. "I'm liking the sound of this. What do you think, Doc?"

Doc scratched his chin for a minute, then stared at me. "Can't say it's foolproof. So much goes wrong in these parts. But it sounds like the thing that makes the most sense."

"Mr. Holiday, how good are you at climbing?" Woody asked.

And that's how I ended up tromping my way up a steep hill wearing tennis shoes. I cursed for not thinking to wear boots or something, but shit, it was spring for God's sake. I wasn't a teenage goth. Though, I kind of missed seeing them around back in the day. Now, so many people looked like carbon copies of each other.

Every couple of steps, my shoes slipped on the grass. I made sure to hold onto various trees and shrubs so I wouldn't slip down the hill. But to be honest, it was close. Tabby and Woody had done a ton of casting on me to make me invisible to wards. While they distracted the witch on the other side, the idea was for me to call to the baby and get it to come to a window so I could befriend it. Not the best of plans, but it was better than nothing.

By the time I crested the hill, a lot of screaming and yelling was happening. I was out of breath. Too much time spent lounging around and not enough getting my ass moving. That needed to change. I heard Tabby and Woody's voices along with the witch, as I expected. Doc stayed back at the house as an extra protection for Lucy's box. Plus, it kept the witch from doing anything with him. We didn't need another ghost to fix. And he'd already had one bad experience with her. Best to leave it all alone.

I crept up to the back side of the house and peered into one of the windows. No baby. Nothing except dust on a little bit of furniture. I moved to another window in what I guessed was yet another room. Still no baby. This was not looking good. I hadn't wanted to move around the house too much because of the discovery risk, but I didn't have a whole lot of choices. The little booger was being too discreet.

I went around the next corner, and I could go no further. If I stepped much more, all the witch would have to do is spin around to see me. I had to face the possibility of this being yet another epic fail.

"Hey there...Hey in there. How are you today?" I spoke softly and what I hoped to be friendly. I tried to angle my head toward the window. I didn't even know if the baby was in this room either, but it was my last shot.

"I need a new friend. No one loves me anymore."

Finally, something moved inside the house. I wanted to pump my fist in the air, but I restrained myself. I was such a dork.

"I need a good friend. Someone who would like to play and run around."

Something hissed. I angled my head and saw the baby staring at me upside down from the open window. Like Doc had described, it had little horn bumps and red eyes.

"Hey there," I said, forcing a smile. The little shit was the weirdest thing I'd laid my eyes on, and I'd seen a thing or two.

The baby grinned back, revealing long tiger-like fangs.

I let my smile grow bigger. "Would you like to by my friend?"

It climbed down the side of the window. Its claws appeared like they could lay me open in a nanosecond. It was too late to worry now. The chances of me coming out of this without a few scars drastically diminished.

"What cute little horns you have."

The baby leapt from the window and into my arms. He was heavy, like someone had tossed me a bag of potatoes.

"Next time, warn me because I wouldn't want to drop you. You're my friend, and I wouldn't want you to get hurt."

The baby drooled and smacked its hands together. Something slinked against my arm. Kid had a tail with a pointed tip. I refocused my attention on his face.

"You are something else, you know that?"

The baby grinned.

"Want to go see what all that noise is about?" I asked the baby. The yelling had reached an almost inhuman pitch.

It squealed.

"Okay!" I was somehow pulling this off. How, I didn't know. To me, I sounded ridiculous.

We walked from around the side of the house. I walked, and the baby traveled in my arms. Woody was holding up her hand in a claw while Tabby and the witch kept yelling at each other. It wasn't a pretty scene.

The baby squealed in my arms and started flailing. It took everything not to drop him. "Settle down, bud."

The witch whipped around.

"Look who jumped out of the window out back. Thank goodness I was there. This cutie could have gotten hurt!" I leaned down and nuzzled his nose with mine. He giggled.

The witch's eyes narrowed. "Give him to me."

I bounced him a little bit, and he drooled. "Oh, come on. He and I were making friends."

"Ezekiel, come here!" She stomped her foot. Not sure what she expected. It wasn't like the little guy had wings and could fly.

Ezekiel buried his head into my shoulder.

I stared at her. "Doesn't look like he's ready to go yet."

She gnashed her teeth.

The way she acted concerned me more than him being unhuman. That was a problem. "Besides, what harm is there? He's safe, getting some sunlight, and he's in your sight."

"You aren't going to like me when I'm angry, Mr. Holiday," the witch said. Her voice had taken on a darkness I hadn't heard before now.

"Don't get angry then. I think he's cute. I would never hurt him." I meant it too. Even a demon baby was a baby animal. Maybe that made me stupid, but I never would have the blood of a child on my hands. Didn't matter where that kid came from.

"What is it you want?" she asked.

Now that the volley was in my court, I might as well take advantage of it. "It would be nice to have our Lucy back to normal."

The witch started to laugh. "I can't fix that."

"Of course you can," Tabby shouted. "You made her that way."

The witch glared at Tabby. "I've about had enough of you."

"No threats, now," I said. "We don't want Ezekiel to get all upset." I didn't feel it was an empty threat. The kid could be capable of anything for all I knew.

She turned back around. "I can't fix what I did not break. She got upset once she learned that there was no way I could give her a body since I had born Ezekiel."

On one hand, I believed her. On the other, I could not imagine Lucy entering a demon baby. It made no sense. Lucy didn't like demons.

"Tabby," I said.

At the sound of her name, Tabby threw a lasso around the witch's waist and pulled tight. The witch went wide-eyed when Tabby allowed her to take the rope. We'd come up with the secret weapon taken from our little string trick. It was meant for keeping things that would do us harm out of rooms when there was very little time to do any major spell work.

"What is this?" she asked.

"A truth spell," Tabby said. "A modified version of another spell I developed. The rope is only symbolic though. You no longer have the ability to lie."

"Forever?" The witch twitched.

Tabby shrugged. "Guess time will tell."

The witch screamed. Ezekiel whimpered.

I patted him on the back. "It's okay. Mommy is upset. It will be all right. I'll protect you."

"Now, fix Lucy!" Tabby edged closer.

The witch laughed again. "I cannot…"

"What are you talking about?" I asked. It couldn't go down like this. Too much hedged on it.

"It wasn't a spell that changed her. It was one of them!" She cackled.

Not good. "Then how do we get her back?"

The witch shook her head. "You need to talk to someone who knows more than I."

"How much more?"

She sighed softly. "You know."

"Shit!" I was not and would not directly call the Devil ever again. Big Red was better off left alone. And if I hadn't learned anything from the last year, it was that. But after this was all put in a box somewhere, I was asking for a vacation.

Ezekiel whimpered.

"I'm sorry, little buddy. I didn't mean to scare you." I patted his shoulder gently.

He settled back down into my chest. Now I was in a pickle. I didn't know what to do with this kid, I didn't know what to do with the Order, and I sure as hell didn't know what to do about Lucy. I was so seriously fucked.

I looked at him. He did seem peaceful. With no claim to him, however, I needed to put things back to normal. "You ready to go back to your mama now?"

He nodded against me.

I walked over to her, a careful step at a time, watching so I didn't step on his tail. He was almost like one of those hairless rats they use in scientific facilities. Weird but cute.

When I got close enough, I handed him to her.

"Are you happy now, Mr. Holiday?" she asked.

"Nope. This ain't over." I paused for a moment to let it sink in, then I joined up with Tabby and lumbered down the hill. Woody trailed behind us.

Doc was sitting at the table when we got down to Woody's. The whole thing had entered a whole new level of screwed up. I kept thinking it couldn't get any worse, and I was proven wrong time and time again.

"Not good, I take it?" he asked.

"No."

I threw into one of the chairs and watched the others come inside. Something about it all left me feeling grumpy and wanting to stay in my bed for days. Obviously, that was not an option.

"You never should have given him to her." Tabby wagged her finger at me.

"And what was I going to do? He isn't my kid. I know nothing about taking care of a baby and this damn mess..." I was starting to get a splitting headache, and if something didn't give soon, I was going to blow.

"Don't give up hope," Woody offered.

I stared at her incredulously. "I take it you have other ideas?"

Woody smiled. "I always have other ideas."

"What is your suggestion?" Tabby asked.

Woody put her hands on her hips and sighed. "Will you calm down for a minute. I'm old, not immortal."

"Sorry." I put my head in my hands. "We're used to

launching one attack right after another." I knew my brain didn't work normally and I tended to bounce from one thing to the next pretty quickly.

"And in a few years, you're going to give yourself a heart attack." Woody rubbed the back of her neck.

"Why don't I put us together some lunch? Woody, just tell me where things are. You go ahead and sit down and rest." Tabby patted the back of the empty chair.

Woody smiled and lowered herself into the chair gracefully. "Now, Tabby, should be some cold cuts in the fridge along with some cheese. Let me know if you need help finding things."

"Sounds good," Tabby said, pulling things out of the refrigerator.

"Now, I think we need to talk to Miss Lucy ourselves to find out what happened so we can get some clue how to fix things." Woody inclined her chin toward me.

Doc said nothing. He seemed defeated. Nothing like the man I knew.

I nodded. "I should try to call that Bishop again to make sure."

Doc cleared his throat.

"What?" I asked.

"Made friends with that thing up there, did you?" He scratched at his chin as if to clear things between his stubble.

"Yeah, why?"

He smirked. "What is it do you think they're going to do to it?"

"What do you mean?"

Doc turned toward Tabby, then focused his gaze back at me. "The church ain't known to keep abominations, you know. They usually kill them—after they torture them for information, that is."

I froze. He was right. The Church wasn't happiness and daisies. They'd been doing some pretty messed up crap for a very long time. Spanish Inquisition, anyone? "Okay. No church after all. But we can't let that woman up there raise it."

"I should hope not," Woody said.

Tabby put a ham and cheese sandwich in front of me. "We can't keep it," she said. "There's no way to explain it. Besides, what would we do when it starts getting big? We've talked about this."

"Yeah, we have. And you said I couldn't give it back to its father." The whole part about it being a bad idea on all accounts to summon Big Red.

"It's impossible." Tabby slapped a piece of meat on a slice of bread.

"Might be more humane to kill it," Doc said.

I gulped. "I promised it I would never hurt it."

Tabby put another sandwich in front of Woody and then sat and set one in front of herself. "I don't even want to think about the size of a cage that thing would need. And the minute anyone saw it and realized it wasn't a joke, some government agency would take it and do the same shit the church would."

I let my head fall into my sandwich. None of this was helping.

"If we get rid of the witch, I could keep it," Woody said, ignoring me.

I raised my chin and stared at her. The top piece of bread fell off my forehead and back onto my plate. "Are you serious?"

She nodded. "Nobody comes out here, so the chances of it being discovered are pretty small. And maybe if it's raised right, it wouldn't be all that mean. The way it took to you was proof."

"Wait a minute. This seems too easy," I said.

Woody blinked.

"I mean, at first, you were all against this. Now, you are acting like we should keep the kid for ourselves. Kind of inconsistent, you know?"

Woody sighed. "I am trying to help you out of this mess you

have gotten yourself in. If you want to try something else, fine. I adapt. If that makes you untrusting of me, I cannot help it."

I wasn't sure if I'd put my foot in my mouth or not, but I couldn't just follow blindly. "I don't mean to be disrespectful."

Woody nodded slowly. "Just remember which of the two who live on this hill have not tried to harm you in any fashion."

She had a point. "If that's the way you want it."

"You're forgetting something," Tabby said.

I blew ham out of my eyes. "What?"

"The Order."

Shit, she was right. I was supposed to do what I always did when a case ended. It required a written documentation of the events before they closed it. I couldn't imagine writing all this down. "I'll have to lie. They've lied to me enough."

"It isn't the first time. Be careful." Tabby patted my hand.

I grabbed what was left of my sandwich off my head and shoved it into my mouth.

After lunch, we went back to spellroom. This time, the only thing in the center of the circle was Lucy's box. I'd already broken the wax seal on it at Woody's direction. Nothing would shake the bad feeling I had. Lucy was now an unknown. It wasn't a good sign.

"Now what?" I asked.

"Might be a good idea to pray," Woody said.

I didn't like the sound of that. It wasn't good when the only advice for an exorcist is to tell him to pray. I needed a drink. If I survived this mess, I was going to need to start carrying supplies with me. Being sober and dealing with all of this was doing things to my brain. I closed my eyes and prayed anyway. "Dear God, please help us make Lucy all right. I know I'm not the best keeper for her, but I do love her like my own. Please, give us the tools we need to make everything okay. Amen."

I opened my eyes, and Woody clapped her hands together over her head so that they resembled a steeple.

"Let's begin." She lowered her arms and rang a little bell. "Lucy, hear me. Come up from the deep."

She rang the bell again. "Come into the light of the world. We are waiting for you."

Woody started to ring the bell a third time when the lid of the box crept opened. It reminded me of a stop motion animation. Kind of jerky and slightly unbelievable.

Lucy appeared in a flash, pressed against the boundary of the circle.

She glared at me and growled. "I don't like being put in a box."

"What happened, Lucy?" Tabby bent low to meet her eyes.

Lucy turned her head toward Tabby. Her eyes were a little less intense. "I got to see where they live."

"They who, honey?" Tabby asked.

"The ones you've been keeping me from all along."

My butthole clenched shut. This was it. Proof that the demonic influenced her. But free will extended into the spirit— otherwise they would have taken Doc too. They capitalized on Lucy's childish desires and her tendency toward anger.

"Only because they hurt you," I said.

Her head whipped around to face me. Her eyes shone back to their scary light. "You hurt me too."

I closed my eyes. "I didn't mean to."

The last thing I had ever wanted to do was hurt her. Life was horrible enough as it was without making her more unhappy than she already was. Her soul had been through too much in a short span of time. Though, for someone her age, it had to feel like forever.

"It doesn't matter," she said.

"Yes, it does, Lucy." Tabby reached a hand out toward her. "The others want to hurt you and cause you pain."

Lucy grinned darkly, ignoring her hand. "They taught me how to cause pain too."

I gulped. She was so beyond the child I knew I barely recognized her. What had happened in Italy had been a blip in comparison. "What happened to you?"

"She brought one to me and left me alone with it while I was trapped."

I wanted to string that witch up and beat her with her own broom. "Oh, honey," I said. "I'm so sorry."

Lucy purged the evil look and shook herself. "I'm not right anymore, am I?"

I sighed. I didn't want to tell her there was probably no going back. I couldn't trust her. And as shitty as it sounded, I wasn't willing to take the risk.

"Maybe I should be dead." She dropped to the floor and set her chin on her knees.

I didn't even know what was an act anymore. "We don't get to make that choice. God decides that."

"I hate God."

Tabby and I both froze.

Woody coughed. "Child, don't hate on God. He created this world, but some things are even out of his control."

"I still hate him." She snarled.

I didn't know if that could be fixed either. I had more pressing things to deal with than her hatred of the higher power. "Let's talk about that more later," I said. "Now, why did you try to kill me?"

She grinned at me. "The lady up there told me that if I did that, I could get my body back."

The poor kid had no idea the extent to which she'd been deceived. It was bad. Real bad. "She lied, Lucy."

Lucy burst into tears. Part of me wanted to hug her, but I wasn't that stupid. The last time hadn't worked out so great.

And probably, if she hadn't tried to kill me, I would have hugged her. With it being me, though, I didn't trust anything. Some might have said I was being too hard on her, but they didn't almost have a knife launched into their spine.

"Lucy?" Doc said from the doorway. His hat was still off his head and his white hair was slicked back from his face with some type of grease. From his era, probably a sort of animal or vegetable fat.

Our plan was for him to stay outside like before. Guess he had other ideas. I didn't want to think about what would happen if her demonic influence rubbed off on him. He was the most powerful spirit I had ever personally encountered.

"Doc!" She jumped up.

He walked over and pressed himself against the circle. His eyes had a stern cast to them. "You did a very bad thing."

Her eyes welled with tears. "I know, but I'm sorry."

He nodded solemnly. "Sometimes, honey, sorry don't cut it."

She bawled harder. No tears were going to make me change my mind. I think Doc knew that.

"Jesus, Jimmy. Can we let her out of there?" Tabby asked.

I glared at her. "No, we cannot. You know better. Doesn't matter what she was before. You aren't thinking straight. I'll be looking over my shoulder every five minutes. She can either stay like she is, if Woody doesn't mind, or she can go back in the box. I have enough to worry about without the possibility of her literally stabbing me in the back."

"That's so cold," Tabby said.

"But smart." Woody opened the door to the room. "She can stay like that for now anyway."

I stared up at her. "Thank you."

Tabby stayed in the room with Lucy. I knew she was pissed at me, but I was beyond caring. I left the room. Maybe there was something wrong with me, but now that the girl I risked my neck for had tried to kill me, I didn't care so much anymore. I would protect her, but I wished God would hurry up and claim her. People would probably hate me for that—Tabby included, but I couldn't help it. I wasn't the forgiving type, and God knew it. Why he chose me to be an exorcist and a Marker was beyond me. I was not the holiest of men.

"Stop wallowing." Woody pulled me from my self-pity.

"Is that what I was doing?"

"That's what it looked like." She grunted. "You have a right to be mad. I would be too."

"Would you let her out?"

Woody shook her head. "No. A spirit with bloodlust is a dangerous thing. She's best off where she's at."

I nodded.

She stepped closer and leaned toward me so that my nose was almost touching hers. "In fact, I'd leave her in the box. Keep a new name for her; one different than even the one you gave her before. And never give anyone else the name, even that girl in the other room. Let God claim her when he's ready."

I stepped back and held out my hand so she could shake it. "We'll do it tonight after she's asleep."

Woody complied. "And then I will put her in a safe place."

"I don't know how we lucked out with you, but I'm glad you're here."

She smiled sadly. "The Lord sure does work in mysterious ways."

Tabby didn't even come in for dinner. Doc joined us for a while. At least I knew he wasn't mad at me. Of course, Doc knew a heck of a lot more about what happened up there in that house than Tabby did. He'd seen it all. Tabby could easily ignore things that were just words. And to be honest, I think she felt some sort of comradery with Lucy. Even though Lucy had tried to kill me, Tabby could dismiss it out of hand. This whole situation sucked. I wished it would hurry up so I could go home and then worry about whether I was getting married after all. It wasn't looking likely.

Tabby did come to sleep on the couch. I waited until I saw her chest rising and falling until I crept back to the spellroom. Woody met me outside the door, then gently placed a tied knotted string with some herbs woven into it on the floor behind me.

"Whew. Now, no sound will carry out there." She placed her hands on her hips.

"You are going to have to teach me that little trick," I said.

"Hopefully, you won't need it." She opened the door to the spellroom, and Lucy stared at us sadly from her place in the middle of the circle.

I figured she thought if she gave me puppy dog eyes, I would set her free. But that didn't work on me

"You're gonna make me go away, ain't you?" Lucy asked. Her eyes dropped the sad demeanor. Now, they just seemed annoyed.

I shook my head. "Going to put you back in the box is all. Things are about to get shaky and I can't risk them getting a hold of you again."

She nodded without making a complaint. Either she was resigned to the whole thing or she had a good idea how bad things were going to get. Either option wasn't great.

I glanced over at Woody, and then began chanting. I extended my Marker voice and called her Lily. I said it so softly that only myself and God could hear. Or that's how I thought of it. I didn't know if Woody had supersonic hearing or anything, but I didn't think that would be a problem. Something told me it would be safe. Either way, this was the best I could do. I closed my eyes and took a deep breath. "I bind you, Lily, inside this box. Never to be opened, unless by my soul or that of God."

I felt tears fall down my cheeks. I would never talk to or see Lucy again. It was shitty and it hurt. I was a bastard.

"You can open your eyes now." Woody tapped my shoulder lightly. "It is done."

I stood up and felt arms around me. I recognized the scent. I hadn't been quite as alone as I had thought. "I'm so sorry, Tabby."

"I am too. When we get home, we'll put her in her room."

I breathed in her scent and tried to relax. Knowing she understood meant more than I thought it would. "Yeah. At least then she'll be in a place that gave her good memories." I turned to face her. "What about Doc?"

I knew he was not going to be happy, but he also knew how bad things were. I hated making him so unhappy. If I had known this whole mess was going to turn into such a shit storm, I would have refused the case. It was all my fault.

TWELVE

ESCAPE

BY MORNING, Doc was gone. I had no idea when he'd left, but I couldn't blame him. I'd taken away the reason he'd stuck around anyway. I knew he wasn't there for me. I wasn't that interesting. And now, we'd gotten to be as dangerous to him as Lucy had been to me. I'm pretty sure he had no desire to be stuck in a box.

Everything felt empty without them though. I missed worrying about Lucy watching her horror movies. I missed Doc's wisdom and sardonic comments. A part of me really felt like a shit. Everything was so wrong at this point that I had no idea which direction to go. I knew the Order wasn't it. And as much as it made me sick, I had to admit that even though I knew what the church would do with Ezekiel, they were the experts with this sort of thing. Maybe it wasn't a good idea to let him live. I didn't know anything.

I stepped onto the back porch and took a deep breath. On the steps laid a piece of old cloth that seemed suspiciously like something from the grave. I did not pick it up. I did not get close enough to smell it. There was no telling what was on that cloth in terms of bacteria, let alone something the witch could have created.

I shook those thoughts from my mind and fished my phone from my pocket. Once again, I dialed the Bishop. "You have reached the Archdiocese of Kentucky. Our operating hours are 9 a.m. to 5 p.m. Monday through Friday. Please leave a message and we'll get back to you as soon as possible."

I wanted to slam my head into the side of the house. Not that it would've solved anything. I waited for the beep. "Yes, I've been trying to get through for a couple of days. My name is Jimmy Holiday. Father Montgomery said that the Bishop would be expecting my call."

I gave my number and hung up. I had now officially done everything I knew I could do. Fate was going to have to take care of the rest. I walked back inside and started a pot of coffee.

Five minutes past nine, my phone rang. I stared at the screen. This was it. I swiped the phone.

"Hello?" I asked.

"Mr. Holiday. We've been having issues with our phone lines. Thank goodness, this morning they seem to have fixed the problem."

Maybe there wasn't anything supernatural surrounding it after all. Too much had happened. I was starting to look for beasties under every rock and leaf. "I agree. I've got a pretty interesting situation here."

I heard him blow his nose. Not exactly the stoic type. Oy.

"That's what I hear," he said. "Now, tell me everything."

I took a deep breath and let it out silently. "I'm from, or was from, the Order of Markers. There is something bad going on there. It doesn't feel trustworthy anymore."

"I see." I could hear some scratching that sounded like a pen against paper. "Go on."

"I was sent down here to investigate a supposed 'devil baby'. They were supposed to have people from the Vatican ready to fly over. They wanted confirmation from me that there was, in fact, a thing and it was real. Conveniently, when I got down here, and got the proof that they requested, there were no experts. They wanted me to take care of it myself. I'm an exorcist, not a creature keeper or whatever you want to call it. I didn't even know if they meant that the kid was possessed or if it was a real, true devil in the flesh sort of thing. At this point, I'm not even sure they knew. None of that matters now because I know. It is real. But when I signed on, it wasn't."

"How good of proof do you have of its authenticity?"

"Only what I saw, but if it helps, I got to hold it in my arms for a half an hour and I can attest to its reality." I still felt my skin crawl at the idea of that tail wrapping around my body.

"I don't know much about this type of thing, but I can call. Let me get back to you."

"Thank you..." I drifted off, not knowing his name.

"Bishop Carl Morris." He filled in.

"I'll look forward to hearing from you." I hung up, then set my phone down on the table. I had a name and someone who was checking into things. It was an improvement.

"What did he say?" Tabby asked.

"He's going to get back to me. But at least he's on it."

Woody pushed a cup of coffee at me.

"Look that bad, do I?" I asked her.

Woody snorted. "Boy, you look like you've been on a week-long bender."

I laughed. "I wish that's all it was."

"I don't ever again want to hear anyone saying that their week has been hell." Tabby sighed.

Woody patted her on the shoulder. "God only gives us what we can handle, and he knows at what point we surprise ourselves."

"And it gets worse before it gets better." I stared down into my coffee cup. Even I didn't believe that. I knew the hits were going to keep coming. It was just a matter of what was next. The only luck I had was bad.

With nothing else to do, we helped Woody clean her house. The only room we didn't touch was the spellroom, for obvious reasons. At least this way we paid for our upkeep a little. There was only so much you could do when someone refused money. Not very many like that these days. In a way, it was a welcome change.

As I had the toilet brush in the bowl, my phone rang again. I didn't take the time to look and just answered it.

"Hello?"

"Mr. Holiday. Sorry it took a bit to get back to you."

Thank God. While I did find it funny I was standing with a plunger in my hand, I was still glad that he got back to me as fast as he could. It was a nice change of pace. "That's okay, Bishop Edwards. What's the decision?"

"The expert no longer travels. He will be glad to take the child, however."

I wasn't sure what to make of that, but it was better than what I knew to do. "Am I to bring him or what?"

He chuckled. "Oh, no. They are sending a team to collect the child. If you would be so kind to email me the directions, I would be quite grateful."

"Not a problem, Bishop Edwards. And thanks for your help."

"No, thank you, Mr. Holiday. We need more to fight the good fight."

He hung up.

I stuffed my phone back in my pocket and finished cleaning the toilet, then I copy and pasted the info I had in my email into a new one and sent it to Bishop Edwards. After that, I went out to the living room where Tabby and Woody were sitting. Tabby on the sofa and Woody in her chair. Guess I was the slow poke of the bunch.

SORROW'S LIE   89

"Bishop is sending a team to collect Ezekiel," I said to them.

Tabby searched my face. "That's going to be interesting."

"We'll have to kill her." Woody adjusted her hands in her lap.

I jerked. "What?"

Woody nodded. "She won't give up that child easily. And those priests will likely need our help. Especially if they come after dark."

"They wouldn't be that stupid would they?" Tabby asked.

I shrugged. I'd seen a lot of things in the church that made me scratch my head. "Depends on how crazy they are and when they get here. The Bishop didn't say where they were coming from."

"We will have to do the best we can." Woody got up from her chair. "We can't risk not allowing the security after dark. I'm sure that the witch has her own plans. But if the priests got here in time, we can protect them."

I blinked. "With what?"

"Goofer dust."

"Oh no," Tabby collapsed into the back of the couch.

I looked back and forth between them. "I'm missing something here."

Woody pointed out the window. "We need to go to the cemetery."

It made me question how weird things could get. "And what do we do up there?"

Woody smiled. "I'll show you. Won't take too long." She put on a pair of old boots and grabbed a paintbrush and a jar. "Come on, now."

Tabby and I had to rush to catch up to her. I was barely able to get the door to the house closed behind me.

We traipsed through the woods on the other side of Woody's house. Down a little hill emerged a path worn in the grass. The path led up a knoll and tapped out at a small cemetery. You could see the entire area from where we stood. Right below us was the witch's house. On the other side of the hill was Woody's.

From up here, the proximity of the houses was even closer than they appeared down below. There must have only been maybe thirty graves. Too many for one family and too small for a town. The more I ogled, the stranger the cemetery seemed.

"What is this?" I asked.

"Unhallowed ground," Woody replied. She leaned into her hip and wiped her forehead with the back of her hand.

"What?"

"This is what you call an outcast's cemetery, Jimmy." Tabby walked next to me. "In earlier times, people who had deformities, or were misunderstood, or performed criminal acts deemed un-Christian were buried in places like this."

"Which is why we use them for ritual purposes." Woody handed me the paintbrush and the jar. "Not rituals here. Nothing unusual. Clean materials so to speak." She glanced at both Tabby and me. "Get to it," she said. "Collect the dust from the top of all the headstones. I haven't collected in a while; should be plenty."

I could honestly say I'd never been asked to do something like that before. But then this wasn't exactly the type of magic Tabby did either. I had a feeling we both were kind of stumbling around in the dark.

"Stop lollygagging, Mr. Holiday."

I saluted Woody. "Yes, ma'am."

It wasn't hard, but it was tricky to get the dust in the jar without spilling it. I ended up doing a combination of brushing the dirt into a pile and scooping the dust into my hands, then pouring it into the jar. A dust pan would have been fabulous. But I guess she didn't have one the right size.

"What's this supposed to do, anyway?" I figured I had a right to know.

"It gives us a bit of power over the dead." Woody picked a few flowers next to one of the graves.

I scratched my head. Instead of giving me answers, that gave me more questions. "What are we doing this for?"

"We are making goofer dust."

I raised a brow. "You said that, but I have no idea what that means."

"Doesn't that kill people?" Tabby asked.

Woody shook her head. "Not unless you spell it to do that. In this case, I'm hoping to spell the priests so that the dead don't see them."

"Wouldn't graveyard dirt do that by itself?" Tabby grabbed a piece of her hair and tucked it behind her ear.

"We don't want them thinking the priests are one of them, that would be bad. Very bad. We need them invisible to the dead."

"Permanently?" I asked.

Woody sighed. "Of course not. Just as long as they don't do something stupid, like put their hands in their mouths after we dust them, they should be fine."

That didn't sound very good. "Will this ritual still work?"

She shrugged. "It should, so long as they really are holy men."

And that was what I feared. I knew enough about the church to know that not all priests were holy men. In fact, some could be downright evil. And there was no way of knowing who was coming. I had to have faith it would all work out, but it was hard. Not much had gone right since I'd been down here.

"That should be enough," Woody said, standing over me.

I stood and handed her the jar. She screwed on the lid and took the paintbrush from me. Then, she started back down the hill without another word.

I grabbed Tabby as she passed. This was really getting to me. I was going to snap soon if I didn't get some answers.

"What?" Tabby asked.

"I don't like the idea of messing with these priests." The part that bothered me most was that Woody didn't want them to put their fingers in their mouths. Meant this shit was dangerous.

Tabby sighed. "I understand feeling untrusting right now, but Woody hasn't led us down the wrong path yet."

I sighed. It wasn't what I meant. I just didn't know if this was smart given how great I had done with actual priests lately. "I know. Just be careful."

She hugged me. "Let's go before she thinks something is up."

Back at the house, Woody led us into the spelling room. She didn't ask where Tabby and I had been, but I figured she knew anyway. She didn't act any differently toward me though, and for that, I was thankful. She probably thought half of my suggestions were weird. The time in her presence hadn't been enough time to get to know each other.

Isaac rubbed against my leg as I passed him into the spell-room. He stayed out of there though. Either he didn't feel wanted or it was because it didn't belong to Tabby. Tabby didn't bring him in either.

"All right you two. Be careful in here. Some of the ingredients are toxic, so you don't want to ingest it." She took a big mortar and pestle from a shelf, grabbed a jar of snake heads, something called magnetic sand, salt, pepper, and a yellow powder in a jar marked sulfur. She also had my jar-o-dirt. Turning to us, her face was stoic and strong and held a different light than I had seen before—a different Woody. "Tabatha is right. Goofer dust can be used to kill. I have never used it for that purpose. I've tried to keep my working toward the light, only using the dark when needed."

Tabby nodded. "The dark never turns out well. I don't care what lies they try to tell you."

Woody motioned to her. "Now, pull me the head of a venomous snake from the jar there."

"How do I know which one is venomous?" Tabby asked.

"Diamond shaped head," I said.

Woody smiled at me. "Maybe I should have you choose."

I shrugged. "My dad got me this collection of snake cards when I was a kid. Didn't want me playing in the woods and get bit for doing something stupid."

It had been one of the good things I remembered about my father. He'd actually stayed sober enough to go through all the cards with me. Usually, he spent the day drinking until he passed out. He was never mean, just not there. For the cards, however, he held off so he could make sure I understood what all the words meant.

"Come over here and help me," Tabby said.

I glanced down into the jar and grabbed a snake head out of it. "This one work?"

Woody nodded. "Put it in the mortar please."

I dropped it in unceremoniously. In a way, I should have felt something for what had once been a living thing. But today, I really wanted to get all this over with.

Woody slammed the pestle into the snake head. It crunched and took her a long time to grind that head into dust. Every so often, she would point at a jar and Tabby would put in the amount from it that Woody had indicated. Finally, Woody passed it all into another jar and placed it on the shelf.

She wiped her hands at last. "Let's all wash up and rest."

I checked my phone. Nothing. All we could do was wait. It would be different if we could do something else with Ezekiel, but we couldn't. This wasn't some mutant movie. It was real life. Then again, my real life wasn't normal per se, but that was beside the point. I wasn't equipped for a baby, let alone a supernatural one. I could barely take care of myself, and that was questionable.

Tabby walked in after her shower and sat at the table, braiding her hair. "What are you going to do about the Order?"

Admitting it had been hard, but now, after all the horseshit, I was done. "Once we get home and safe, I'm going to turn in my resignation. If God wants me to continue being a Marker, he will give me the resources. Otherwise, I'll have to find another line of work."

Tabby threw the tail of her hair over her shoulder. "You could always go back to school."

I laughed. "Because we both know how great that turned out."

She snorted coffee through her nose, then dabbed at everything with a napkin. While still laughing, she said, "Or you could have your own TV show."

I shook my head. "Nah. No way would I abuse the power like that. It wouldn't be right."

It probably made me a sap, but if I didn't keep my principles, there wasn't much left. I could have a much different life, but I was sure eventually God would get pissed off and take my power away anyway.

Tabby took my hand in hers. "And that's why I love you. Even though you are about to be out of a job with no money, you hold onto your principles."

I shrugged. "Part of it is a good healthy fear of God and what he might do to me."

She laughed. "If that were the case, I think you would have treated the exorcism school with more respect."

"No reason to respect what does not respect you," Woody said from the doorway.

I looked up. "Either you're psychic or you know someone who is feeding you information about me."

Woody chuckled. "Maybe a bit of both."

"Nothing surprises me." I squeezed Tabby's hand. "What should I do?"

Woody lowered herself in the chair next to Tabby. "I've never been the type to tell people what to do."

I snickered.

Isaac meowed from the floor near the stove. I gave him a thumbs up.

Woody crossed her arms. "I realize that's surprising, but it's true. Not my fault if people do not listen to my advice."

"That's how I feel," Tabby said.

"Okay. What would you do in my shoes?"

Tabby stared at me. "Not rush to results. You have no idea who is watching the ones watching you. Could be, they are waiting for them to bury themselves."

"True." I sighed.

"And so far, you have come out okay."

I shoved a hand through my hair, thinking about the losses. "Minus Doc and Lucy."

"But they didn't know about them, did they?" Woody asked.

"Not as far as we know." Tabby let go of my hand to run her fingers over her braid. "But it has put us in a bind with Lucy's father. I don't know if he can take losing her again."

I wanted to throw myself off a bridge. While I hadn't forgotten about Wil, I sure as hell didn't have him on my mind. "Great. Give me something else to worry about. Thanks, Tabby."

She smiled sadly. "You're welcome."

My phone vibrated on the table. I wanted to chuck it across the room. Instead, I read the text message:

Mr. Holiday. I've been told that the crew is on its way. They should reach you in a couple of hours. I have given them your phone number. They are to contact you before going to the house for background.

I texted back. *Sounds good. Thank you for letting me know.*

"Well?" Tabby asked.

It was on, but I wasn't sure how I felt about it. If it wasn't for the fact that I was pretty sure Woody didn't have any alcohol, I would have taken the nearest bottle. "They will be here in a few hours."

Woody glanced at the clock. "It will be close. But if they are on time, we should be able to dust them."

"And if we don't have enough time?" I asked. All of our

work on that dust stuff would have been wasted, not to mention that I didn't like the thought of that witch and Ezekiel and what they could do after dark.

Woody stared at me—hard. "Better get ready to fight some zombies."

THIRTEEN
ATTACK

TWO HOURS LATER, still no car. I cursed under my breath. I didn't even want to see a real zombie, let alone fight one. The bacteria factor alone freaked me. And the teeth factor. Most importantly, I couldn't exorcize a zombie. Their animated flesh was like a parasite, not a possessed being. If the movies were right. If they were wrong, I would know what to do. That would be a first.

"Why can't they ever be on time," I mumbled.

Tabby sighed. "Because they don't take this seriously. They probably don't even believe that Ezekiel exists. I would imagine they stopped and ate, stuff like that."

"Part of me is tempted to let the zombies get them." And film it and put it online, but I didn't say that aloud.

Isaac meowed under the table. I reached down and he trotted over. I scratched him behind the ears for a minute. "See? He agrees with me."

My phone rang, interrupting the petting session.

"Hello?" I said into the cell.

"Mr. Holiday?" the voice asked.

"Yes."

"I hear you are harboring something unusual."

If this was how this was going to go, I was not having it. I had better shit to do with my time. "I'm not harboring anything. It lives up the road with its mother."

The guy on the phone choked.

Now maybe the idiot would listen and get something done. "How do you want to do this?"

"I supposed we would come see for ourselves, then address the mother from there."

Pompous ass. He'd see what was up there alright. He wasn't even smart enough to ask himself if all this was a joke. Why should I bother? "If you don't get a move on, you're going to have more to worry about than a devil baby."

"What are you talking about, Mr. Holiday?"

It wouldn't be kind of me not to warn them. If they ran into trouble and someone got hurt, it would not be on my shoulders. "There are zombies in these hills."

He laughed so hard I had to pull the phone away from my ear.

That was it. "You know what? Fuck you. I was trying to help."

I hung up. The whole mess had been hard enough without his bullshit. They could get eaten for all I cared. Screw them.

"What the hell, Jimmy?" Tabby asked.

"Asshole laughed at me. I don't have to take that from anyone." I leaned back in the chair and tried to calm down.

The phone rang again. I picked it up and stared at the screen. It was them. "I'm not answering it."

I threw my phone on the table. Tabby grabbed it.

"Hello," she said. "No, you don't want to speak to him right now. Yes, he was perfectly serious. Ever hear of voudou? Uh-huh."

I was a bit curious what the asshole was saying, but the sadistic part of me wanted to sit on Woody's porch with a beer and watch the show. I was so glad I was no longer a priest. It meant that I didn't have to be nice.

Tabby rolled her eyes. "No, I don't think we can help with that. Yes, have Bishop Montgomery update us. Goodbye."

She handed me my phone. "We are not helping him. He was a total asshole, and something feels wrong."

At least it wasn't just me. I didn't like the dickhead being mean to Tabby, but at least we knew fate would intervene. No way this wouldn't become one hell of a mess for him. I felt the smile curl my lips.

Woody started grabbing pots and pans. "Might as well cook dinner then."

I got up from the table. "Sounds good to me. How can I help?"

I wished I could've said the rest of the night was uneventful, but it wasn't. Something was at work egging all the shit on. If I could've tracked it down and beat its ass, I would have done it. It all started when Woody went outside and did some sort of ritual. I heard chanting, then Woody came inside and smirked.

"Figured we would want to watch the festivities," she said.

I didn't mention how she'd lied about controlling them or the goofer dust. Maybe she wanted the extra help with making the crap. But small inconsistencies didn't matter to me so much. Her actions did. She hadn't done anything to hurt me. Part of me had to wonder, though, if she had anything at all to do with what happened to Doc and Lucy. Granted, she had helped me put the kid in the box, but something else nagged at me. Something that didn't seem to make a lot of sense.

Tabby and I stepped outside. Woody blew dust in our faces. Thank God I hadn't opened my mouth or it would have been more of a mess than I could have fathomed.

"For God's sake, don't breathe it in. That will kill you for sure." Woody stared at us, frozen. Once it became apparent we were okay, she screwed the lid on the jar.

"We needed that?" I asked.

"You did." She pointed into the yard. "How do you think I can keep them from getting agitated? I told you before."

I didn't breathe. Her finger pointed toward an army of corpses that swayed side to side in their own rhythm. I hadn't even realized how dark it had gotten. I'd been so wrapped up with the asshole on the phone and my thoughts that I had forgotten to pay attention.

The zombies resembled mummies, but as they moved, you could hear a rustling. No rotten smell. No oozing wounds. Just corpses. Old corpses covered in flesh dust. As they moved, their skin cracked and flaked.

"Oh. My. God." It came out without me meaning to speak it.

In unison, their faces turned toward me, but all I could see were a sea of eye sockets. While I remained silent, they did not move. After a heartbeat, they went back to swaying.

"See," Woody said. "If they could smell you, they'd be interested. Not good to have the dead interested in you."

I didn't bother to tell her I already had that problem; I kept my mouth shut. "We're okay as long as we don't touch our eyes, breathe it in, or put out fingers in our mouths?"

Woody nodded. "Now, sit down and relax. They still might get agitated from all the noise."

Tabby and I listened and sat on the porch. It wasn't comfortable, but it would do. Ten minutes later, a black SUV rolled up the drive to the witch's house. Four figures hopped out and walked up the steps. We were too far away to hear voices. They didn't even look down the hill toward us. As soon as they reached the door, a struggle occurred.

"You can't have him!" the witch screamed. I could make out her hair flying all over the place as she fought against them.

Her shrill cry carried clear to us. Eventually, they pushed her aside and barged their way into the home. The witch got bounced off the door.

A gunshot rang loose. Then, the sound of something unholy —like the screech of a demonic bird of prey. One of the priests ran out of the house, blood dripping from his head. In unison, all the zombies turned in his direction. I guess the smell of the blood traveled far. I started to speak, but Woody grabbed my arm and shook her head. I turned my attention toward the priest again. The zombies moved forward. Instead of the usual zombie lope, it was almost like the stutter flash you see in Japanese horror films. Soon, Mr. Priest was surrounded by the hoard of animated dead flesh. He screamed. And then they were on him. We could see nothing but a swirling mass of bodies. His screams died out, and all that was left was the wet sound of gnashing teeth.

"They're distracted now. Safe to talk," Woody said.

I swallowed hard.

"This is ghastly," Tabby replied.

"No, this is wrong." I wasn't sure what to do about it. And while I thought the priests were assholes, I hadn't expected them to die. It was horrific in the truest sense of the word. I would never watch a zombie movie the same way again.

Another scream from the house and another gunshot crashed through the air. The next priest staggered from the house with blood running from his stomach.

"Help me!"

The zombies all stood up as one. Their skin wasn't so papery in the dim light. Almost as if the juices of their meal had regenerated them somewhat. The priest fell down the porch steps, and in an instant, they were on him. The only saving grace was that we were too far away to hear the feeding sounds. It did nothing for the visual though.

"This is evil," I whispered.

"No, what was evil was the one who condemned them to

this. If I could find the one, I would break their curse," Woody whispered back.

Another priest was thrown out of an upstairs window. A shriek in the night sounded, anything but human. It came from inside the house.

"What the fuck was that?" I asked, forgetting to whisper.

One zombie stutter-stepped to the porch. His face was plumper and those empty eye sockets stared at me like eyes. He clattered too close for my comfort. Another step and he could reach me. The other zombies seemed to be stutter-stepping raggedly down the hill. They weren't moving in unison like before

I finally saw it, a small figure crawling as fast as it could. This was not happening. I'd reached my limit. "Stop!"

I'd spoken with my Marker voice, not meaning to do it. Something inside me had taken over. All the zombies focused their eye sockets on me. I let my subconscious go and the words flew from my mouth faster than I could think them. "Your spirits are free. You are dead. Find your path away from this world. Leave me and mine alone. Go back to your graves."

Their bodies jerked and then fell over in unison, like unfolded laundry dropping on the floor. A few skulls rolled from their skeletons.

A woman screamed. Something slammed into me and about knocked me off the porch.

Poor Ezekiel was covered in blood, a big scrape on his fore-head. He wrapped his tail around my waist.

"Hell," I said.

The baby clung to me like I was his only safe place left in the world. It broke my heart.

Another gunshot rang up on the hill. I didn't wait around to see what happened to who and carried the baby into the house. He'd seen enough in his short life. I didn't care whether he was human or not.

"Jesus Christ, Jimmy," Tabby said once she and Woody closed and locked the door. She stood there with her arms wrapped around her stomach, staring at me.

"Ain't got protection around the house now. Wards will have to hold," Woody said. She didn't seem too happy and kept starting at Ezekiel.

"I'm sorry about that." I didn't mean to put her in a spot. It seemed like everything I did ended up hurting someone.

Woody wrung her hands together and peered out the kitchen window. Then, she glanced back at me. "Don't worry about it. I wouldn't have let them eat him either."

Ezekiel raised his head and blinked his eyes. Isaac peered from around the cabinet on the floor. Ezekiel cooed. Isaac hissed and ran away.

"That's definitely going to be an interesting dynamic." Cat vs. Demon. Only forty-nine, ninety-five.

"We can't keep him, Jimmy." Tabby swallowed. "We already talked about this."

I glared at her. What was done was done. There were no easy answers. "So I should have let him die?"

She threw her hands in the air. "Of course not! I simply mean we need to figure out what to do now."

I shrugged. Maybe I was getting ahead of myself. Too much stress and not enough sleep. "His mom will be showing up soon, I'm sure."

Ezekiel growled.

I stared at him. His face was all pulled back like he wanted to hiss. "Is your mommy mean to you?"

His face relaxed and he nodded.

That put an end to it. My decision had been made for me. "Okay. You won't go back there."

"I don't like the sound of that," Tabby said.

Woody handed me a clean wet cloth. "Let's clean up that scratch. He'll be fine for the night. We'll give him water to drink. That won't hurt him."

"Am I the only sane one left?" Tabby asked. She glared at each of us in turn.

I gently wiped Ezekiel's head. "Probably."

Having a demon baby that liked you turned out to be pretty damn problematic. No matter what I did, he didn't let me set him down. Once, I had to pee, and Tabby got bit while trying to make him stay out of the bathroom. Woody got her bandaged up okay, but every time Ezekiel got near her, he would hiss and she would glare at him. Isaac stayed hidden. I didn't blame him. Unlike Lucy, this kid could hurt him.

The witch made a few noises outside the house, but nothing more. Woody's wards went farther than I thought. But I didn't want to talk about such things around Ezekiel in case his mother had some sort of spell on him. Whether she treated him poorly or not, I knew it did a lot to a kid's psyche to hear someone else badmouth his mother and I wasn't about to do it. Or at least I'd try not to.

For now, he was safe and that was what mattered. It was the best I could do, but it was a hell of a lot better than the alternative.

The next morning, I woke up feeling wet. I peered down. I had baby demon pee all over me. It smelled like a cross between cat piss and guano. "Ezekiel, we gotta figure out a signal or something, dude."

He stared up at me with those red eyes and smiled. His fangs peeked from below his lip.

"You are too cute, you know that?" I got out of the chair and took him into the bathroom. I set him in the bathtub where he wouldn't get hurt and ran water in the sink to soak my shirt. Luckily, none of the pee had gotten onto Woody's chair.

"Anything wrong, Jimmy?" Tabby asked through the door.

I didn't know where to begin. "Yeah, can you get me a new shirt? Ezekiel had an accident."

I heard the floor creak outside the door. "Sure. I'll see if I have something he won't swim in too. We don't need him getting sick."

A few moments later, Tabby knocked on the door and passed me some clothes. I put on the new shirt after washing Ezekiel and myself off. I made sure to dry him off carefully. Wasn't like we had any powder or anything. We'd have to put down newspapers or something until we were able to get something better.

I came out carrying him. I'd left my wet t-shirt hanging in the bathtub after I'd washed it by hand. Did the same with the shirt Ezekiel had on. Now, we were both clean and dry. No telling how long it would last, but at least we didn't stink.

"Everyone okay?" Woody asked.

I nodded. "Someone's probably hungry. Did anything get ruined?"

"Nothing that a little work won't fix." I glanced outside. Someone had destroyed all of Woody's flowers. They had been a spot of beauty that hadn't harmed anyone. Bunch of bullshit.

"Did the witch do that?" I asked.

Woody grunted. "Most likely."

I sat at the kitchen table and picked up my phone. Multiple texts had come in from the Bishop about the team. Good thing I hadn't checked last night. The mood I'd been in, the poor man would have gotten live video. But he'd been decent, even if the team hadn't. He deserved some answers.

I dialed his number and waited. After a few rings, he answered.

"Oh, thank God, Mr. Holiday. How are things over there?"

I coughed. "With me, fine. With the team, not so much."

I heard him clear his throat. "What do you mean?"

"The devil baby's mother shot a few of them. One got thrown out of an upstairs window, and some were eaten. It wasn't pretty." Wasn't really an easier way to explain that one. It sounded ridiculous.

The Bishop gulped. "Eaten?"

"Yeah." I paused. "By zombies."

"Did you just say what I thought you said?"

"Yup. Not something to worry about. I got rid of the zombies." I knew I was being flippant, but I was done. None of this could be explained in a "normal" way. Everything had gone to shit, and it appeared to be following me. Or, something around me. Who knew at this point. I was running my mouth.

"Did you call the police?" he asked.

I almost laughed. "Seriously, would you?"

He sighed. "Good point."

"Okay, let's focus. I know three bodies were outside the witch's house last night. No idea if she's moved them or not. No idea if the fourth priest is alive or not." I hadn't seen everything. It was highly doubtful he'd survived, but not impossible.

I heard him rustle some papers.

"I guess I better call Rome," he said.

"Might not be a bad idea."

"So?" Tabby asked.

I shrugged. "He's calling Rome. No direction for us, thank God. I think we have more than enough on our plates."

Tabby gingerly reached forward as if to touch Ezekiel. He

snapped at her. She was trying. I had to give her credit for that. But if the little guy didn't watch himself, he would get to see Tabby's dark side. Somehow I didn't think he would like it very much.

I shook my finger in front of his nose. "Now, now. That's not nice. Tabby is going to be my wife. If you wanna hang out with me, you gotta hang out with her too."

He pouted.

While he was cute, no way was I going to give into that—especially not this soon.

"All right, little fella. You have a choice. You can have milk or water," Woody said to Ezekiel.

He blinked at her.

"Okay. Milk it is."

I didn't even bother asking how she knew. I had accepted that Woody had powers I didn't fully understand, and that was nothing new. I didn't even understand my own.

She'd found an eyedropper from somewhere and set it on the counter. Then, she started heating milk on the stove.

"Give me back my baby!" the witch yelled from outside.

I carried Ezekiel to the porch so she could see him. "Why should I? He sure doesn't seem like he wants to go back to you."

In fact, Ezekiel was shivering and had buried his head into my neck. It was warm outside. About seventy. The weather wasn't making him shake like a leaf. Demon baby or not, I sure wasn't going to give him up to her if he was that afraid of her. I wasn't that much of a dick.

"He belongs to me. And he needs to come home."

I shrugged. "Hey, it's not like you can call the police."

Her body became very still. "Don't mock me, Mr. Holiday. I can call lots of things. Now, give me back my son."

I focused on Ezekiel. Little guy's eyes went wide with fear. "Wanna go home?"

He buried his head in my neck further.

I glanced at her. "No can do. Maybe we can figure out visitation."

She grumbled. "Don't say I didn't warn you, Mr. Holiday. I'll be back."

"I'm betting on it."

I watched her storm her way up the hill. Once she had gone inside her house, Ezekiel and I went into Woody's. Tabby and Woody stared at us from their places at the table.

"Did you really pick a fight with a bad witch?" Tabby asked.

I chuckled. "I think I did."

"Oh brother."

Woody brought me a bowl of milk and set the eye dropper next to it. "Why don't you see if you can get that baby fed?"

After I got Ezekiel fed—which was a damn giant mess of warm milk all over us, the table and the floor—I laid him down for a nap on the couch. I was not good at this and we were going through clothes much too fast. I hadn't brought many and I couldn't expect Woody to wash our stuff all the time. This was getting out of hand.

Tabby and Woody cleaned up the kitchen. Isaac helped with the milk on the floor. Apparently, it was okay for milk to have touched a demon baby's mouth, just not for the demon baby to touch him.

I wanted to make sure the baby wouldn't slip off the couch. Things were going to have to change and fast. It was clear now how poorly equipped we were to deal with a baby, let alone a supernatural one.

Either I was going to have to go against my principles and give him back to his mother and tell the Order to fuck off or I was going to have to sacrifice my soul, summon a demon, and tell the Order to fuck off. There was only one thing in either option that I liked.

It wasn't much of a choice. Tabby walked in from the kitchen and threw herself into Woody's chair. "Jesus. That was a job."

"No doubt. Really, I know we need to make different arrangements, but I don't know what." If I even knew someone who wanted children at this point, I would have asked them if they were willing to take on a very special child. But I didn't even have that at my disposal.

"What choice do you have?"

"It's between summoning a demon or giving him back to his mother who I think abuses him."

Tabby sighed. "You'd never be able to look for bruises. That scratch is already gone on his head."

I check over his head. She was right. I hadn't even noticed. Little guy healed fast. "What would you do?"

Tabby leaned back. "Don't ask me that."

I had an idea as to what she meant, but I wanted her to say it. "I take it you have an option number three?"

She ran her hands over her hair. "It's ugly and it's awful, but it solves all the problems."

I nodded. That confirmed it. "That's why he doesn't like you."

She sighed. "I never was good with children."

"I didn't think I was either."

She chuckled. "You think you aren't good at a lot of things that you really are."

"You're probably right."

She stared at Ezekiel for a moment. "What are you going to do?"

I didn't like it, but it was the better option of the two. Maybe his father wouldn't abuse him. "Borrow some stuff from Woody and ask if I can use the graveyard."

"I'll go pack up the car."

"Isn't that a bit cart before the horse?" I was going to try a summoning. It didn't mean we were going to get to leave anytime soon.

She stared at me, then sat back down. "Wishful thinking more like. How are you going to know who to summon?"

"I figured I would google it." I sure wasn't going to ask that witch the name of Ezekiel's father. I figured I might be able to guess in terms of physical features or something. Surely an old woodcut would capture that—at least I hoped so.

"Lovely," Tabby said. She gave me that look. The one she always gave me before I did something really stupid.

Googling demons...not the easiest thing in the world. A lot of video game stuff, fake magic sites, and then I got to the real stuff —about every fifty sites. Who knew demons were that popular?

Too bad, no listing for which demons were more apt to procreate with humans' section. Bet they had them at the Vatican, but I'd burned that bridge. No way would they be willing to share information. I knew better than to even try.

I had no idea what I was going to do. Probably best to admit I was a failure yet again.

"Jimmy?" Tabby was standing over me with her hands on her hips. "Ezekiel wants you. He's in the kitchen on the floor in front of the door and won't let Woody outside."

I jumped up and followed her. When I got into the kitchen, I saw him sitting right in the middle of the doorway. His face was all pinched up like he was ready to cry. His mouth pouted and his fangs poked into his lower lip.

"Hey, bud. What's going on?"

He gave a strange purr-like sound. What I wouldn't give for that kid to be able to speak, but I had to take what I could get.

I peered out the kitchen window. The witch was on the hill, glaring at the house. She was far enough away that she wouldn't be any danger that I could see, but her staring like that was unsettling nonetheless.

"Were you trying to protect Woody?" I asked him.

He scurried over and wrapped his arms around my legs. Poor kid was shaking.

Woody walked over, crouched down, and patted Ezekiel's head. "Don't you worry. We are going to be taking care of this. I appreciate you trying to protect me, but I can do that fine." She looked up at me and then back down at him. "Besides, we will need food from the grocery store soon. We can't stay inside here forever."

I nodded.

Woody stared into the yard. "I'll go outside and re-strengthen the wards later. She can't stand there all day."

I picked up Ezekiel and carried him with me into the living room. He hissed at Tabby as we passed her. She stuck her tongue out at him. In a way, it was funny as hell. If the implications hadn't been so bad, I would have laughed.

It was a heck of a quandary. Not like I could ask Ezekiel about his dad. Kid was smart, but so far, he didn't seem to have any psychic talent. And even then the chances of him being able to focus at such a young age was nil. Especially since he couldn't tell me what was going on in his brain. He was supernatural, not omniscient. The old exorcist, Malachi Martin, used to talk about how the demonic could influence the exorcist's life in ways they never could foresee. But I had to remain focused. I had direct involvement with a little demon. I had no idea where that put me in light of God. Would I now be considered evil because I was trying to protect this kid? Would I be evil getting him help?

I cleared the cache on my phone. Summoning a demon was not the answer. That would damn me in the eyes of God as much as I hadn't wanted to admit it. And since I had already summoned the devil once before, best not to press my luck. I needed to remain as pure as possible. Already, I wasn't the holiest of men.

I set Ezekiel on the floor. "Bud, you need to make friends with Tabby. You might end up staying with us for a while."

What I didn't want to say was that if all this went to shit and I ended up dead, Tabby was the only person who might be able to take care of him safely. She wouldn't be happy, and neither would he, but Woody was too old to take care of a baby, her life extended or not. It was too much work.

He blinked at me and stared. I was getting nowhere.

"I know she can be prickly. But I also know as much as she says it, there is no way she would hurt you."

He gave me a look that seemed like he didn't believe me.

"At least let her help me. I promise I will keep an eye on her."

I knew better than to tell him I would protect him over Tabby. He was part demon after all. That would put me in a strange place and at a disadvantage should an older demon decide to take advantage of it.

He grunted, and I took that for a yes. It wasn't great, but it was a start.

"Lunch time!" Tabby called from the kitchen. I picked up Ezekiel and carried him in. He was good. Didn't squirm.

"Ezekiel has promised to try to be nicer to you," I said to Tabby.

"That would help." Her face was more stoic than Ezekiel's. God help me.

Woody placed another bowl of warm milk next to me and the eyedropper.

"Think you could let him wear this?" She held up a garbage bag with a hole opened up for his head.

"I can try."

After some minor fuss, Ezekiel was covered in the bag and another bag was on the floor under the chair.

"Tabby and I hoped that maybe this could prevent us getting him so messy, since it wasn't like we had many clothes for him."

I felt sorry for him. None of this could be comfortable. "Shame his mother won't cooperate. I'm sure she has lots of stuff up there."

Tabby walked behind me and sat on the side furthest away from Ezekiel. "I don't think so. You said it yourself. Ezekiel is abused." She took a bite of a sandwich in front of her.

It was pretty damn sad that the kid was mistreated. Human or not, he was cute in a strange sort of way. All babies were cute on some level for God's sake. And whether you liked them or not, it didn't give people cart blanche to mistreat them either.

Woody put a garbage bag on me like a backward cape. I felt like I was going to some shock opera. "Okay, Mr. Holiday," she said. "Let's see how this works."

I started giving Ezekiel sips of milk with the eyedropper. This time, it wasn't so bad since I knew how much to put in so he could swallow it. A bit of the milk got spilled, but it was on the plastic. How they were going to keep it from spilling until we got done, I didn't know, but at least it was helping.

Ezekiel squealed and I dropped the eyedropper—luckily just on the table and not on the floor where it would likely have shattered.

I followed his gaze and spied Isaac lapping up the milk from the plastic.

I chuckled. "Like the kitty?"

He clapped his hands under the plastic and started squirming.

I held onto him tighter. "No, we gotta finish lunch. Besides, your claws could hurt kitty."

Ezekiel pouted.

"I know. Maybe we can figure out how to make it safe for both you and kitty."

Even with Isaac's help, the kitchen was still a mess. Most of the milk ended up on the plastic, but some of it still rolled off. Isaac was only one cat after all. We needed to get bottles and an answer.

Ezekiel agreed to let Woody hold him while I ate my sandwich. On one hand, it was kind of cute the kid like me that much. On the other, it made little to no sense. I marked souls to get to God. That was my job. The exorcisms were only part of it. I wasn't complaining though. My arms were hurting from holding him that long. He wasn't light.

"When do you want to begin?" Tabby asked.

"Never? Google-fu failed me."

Tabby sighed. "What are you going to try now?"

I shook my head. "Praying? I haven't tried it, and the other options royally suck."

"Would you give up your soul for him?" Woody asked.

I didn't even have to think about it. "No. I'm not even sure what type of soul he has."

Woody nodded thoughtfully.

"What do you think about an exorcism?" Tabby asked.

I sighed. That's what the Order wanted me to do in the first place, sorta. It really wasn't a good option. "I'm sure it could work, but you didn't see what happened when I exorcized the real demon back in Kitzmiller. Ezekiel would be hurt at the very least. He may even die."

"When it's in them naturally, ain't nothing you can do to get the bad out." Woody creakily got up from the table and started doing the small amount of dishes we'd used.

Her words rang true. Ezekiel didn't have a good future no matter how you sliced it.

"Best you can do," she said, "is try to teach him right from wrong. And even then, most times, the bad takes over."

"How many babies like that have you seen?" Tabby asked.

"Enough. Would have liked not to see any more ever again."

I glanced at Tabby. She shrugged.

I laid my hand on Ezekiel's head and began. "God, Lord of peace, hear my prayer. Give me the strength and knowledge to help this child—"

Someone screamed outside. I jerked my hand from his head. Tabby, Woody, and I jumped up and stared out the window. Ezekiel's mother stood on the porch twitching under the power of the wards.

Fuck.

The fact she could get past them made my blood grow cold.

Woody opened the door and stood there, staring at the woman. Almost as if she was challenging her to come closer.

"Give him back to me," the witch said in between gasps.

"You ain't got no right to be here," Woody said quietly.

"I do. He's my kin." She pointed at Ezekiel.

"And what about the abuse?" I knew I should have let Woody handle things, but I couldn't help it.

The witch opened and closed her mouth several times. "Abuse. What abuse? He doesn't like it when I make him mad."

"What are you talking about?" I was really confused now.

She snarled. "He doesn't like his lessons, but he has to be trained. His father decreed it."

I froze. Not sure what I've been expecting, but this sure was not it. "What lessons?"

"Give him to me," the witch said.

"What is going to happen to him anyway?" I asked partly out of curiosity and partly because I wanted all my ducks in a row. Besides, no way in the world was I handing him over to her voluntarily, no matter what type of fuss she made. She was crazier than a wildebeest that had eaten meat covered in hot sauce.

She grinned. "He will be the one who is foretold. His markings will fade as he ages. Even now, his eyes aren't quite as red as when he was born."

I dared to search his eyes. His irises still seemed pretty damn red to me. Suddenly, she shot a flash of light toward me. Woody put her hand up right in time to block it, but her palm sparked and the room smelled like burnt flesh.

"You bitch." I set Ezekiel on the floor behind me. He scurried away.

Woody stepped in front of me and began chanting. With the end of each sentence, the woman backed further down the steps. I followed Woody onto the porch. The chanting increased. As soon as the witch was outside the wards, she fired back at Woody.

Woody stopped each shot with her hands, but I could tell she was getting tired. The toll on her flesh couldn't have been good either.

"Jimmy, do something," Tabby said from the doorway.

I had no idea what on Earth to do. It wasn't like I knew how to blight people. Jesus. I whipped up my arms and threw out my Marker voice. "I bind you from doing harm against anyone!"

The witch laughed. "You don't even know my real name and you expect to bind me?"

She threw a spell at me and I ducked. It crackled against the side of the house and left a scorch mark.

"Enough!" Woody held out the chicken's foot and pressed it against the witch's arm.

How she'd moved that fast, I didn't know. And I didn't even know where she'd hidden that damn foot either.

"No. No. No. No. No." The witch was trembling and blood poured from her scalp.

From inside the house, I heard Ezekiel scream. Woody ran inside. I glanced back at the witch. Her skin had turned as black as tar and seemed to be burning off her bones. With every minute that passed, another piece of skin curled up and fell to ash. Finally, there was nothing left except for a dark, murky spot in the grass.

That was when a dark SUV pulled into the driveway behind our car. My luck was getting better and better.

"Damn it."

Three priests stepped out of the car and walked forward. The tallest and the closest turned to me. "Did we see what we thought we saw?"

I nodded. "You need to go up there." I pointed toward the witch's house. As soon as they were out of sight, I chanced a glance behind me. Woody stood there.

"What do we do now?" I asked.

"Nothing. What is left can rot where it lays."

I walked passed her, went inside the house, and froze. Tabby was sprawled on the floor with the baby demon at her neck. I didn't hesitate and knocked it away. It screamed. Blood poured from Tabby's neck. She was going to die.

I felt a hand on my arm. My vision altered. I was still standing on the porch.

"You need to get some rest," Woody said. "I think all of this is starting to affect you."

I shook my head, unsure of what I'd seen. "Why's that?"

"You look like you're about to pass out, that's why."

The night air swirled around my body. The vision turned my blood cold, but I didn't mention it. No need to make anyone else off kilter.

I let Woody lead me into the house. Tabby sat at the table. Ezekiel was on the floor, staring at Isaac. Isaac stood about five feet away, staring back. I'd never been more relieved in my life.

"Is everything okay?" Tabby asked. She got up and placed her hand against my forehead.

It felt clammy against my flesh. "I look that bad, do I?"

Woody pushed me into a chair. "I think it was all too much for him. After I killed the witch and the goons from the church showed up, I thought we'd have one heck of a mess on our hands."

Tabby took my head in her hands. "Jimmy, what's wrong?"

I shook myself. "I think I had a vision."

"Of what?"

No way was I going to tell her. She would act worse toward Ezekiel. That we didn't need. "It doesn't matter now. What I saw isn't possible." And it wasn't. I was going to make sure she was never left alone with Ezekiel.

After I'd had a nap in Woody's bed with Ezekiel, I took him with me while I went to the bathroom. Then, I headed for the living room. Tabby sat on the couch with a bunch of shopping bags around her. Woody was in her chair, meticulously clipping sales tags from baby clothes. I hadn't realized I'd slept that long.

"Boy, you have been busy." I rested on the sofa, holding Ezekiel as far away from Tabby as possible. I tried not to make it noticeable, but she stared at me strangely anyway. I forced myself to relax.

"We figured now that things were safe, we'd get what we needed. Including pampers and bottles," Tabby said.

I laughed. "Too afraid to go in the house up there."

"Uh-huh. Call it whatever you want, but I bet you she cursed that house before she died." Woody stared out the window.

"Knowing her, you're probably right." I adjusted Ezekiel on my knee. He remained content enough. I didn't know what to do with him. Any option I could think of had run out.

"Think I should try praying again?" I asked.

"Prayer don't hurt anyone," Woody said as she folded the final pair of baby pants.

"You know one thing you haven't tried?" Tabby asked.

"What?"

"Contacting the Order directly. What if the problem all along has been Father Martin?" Tabby asked.

I sucked in a breath through my teeth. She had a point. The last time I had sent a general email had been ages ago, when I had still been at the exorcism school trying to get a translator. "Only problem is I have no way of contacting them."

Tabby glared at me, clearly exasperated. "You call them—"

I shook my head. "No, I call Father Martin. I still never had a direct line to the Order. And I left the iPad at home, so I don't even have the email address."

Tabby rolled her eyes. "It's your iPad e-mail, right?"

"Yeah?"

"And you know your user name and password?"

I nodded.

"Give me your damn phone."

I dug it out of my pocket and passed it to her.

After a couple minutes of fiddling, she glanced at me. "Username?"

"J holiday eighty-eight at apple dot com."

"Password?"

"Capital G. Little r–e–e–n-8-8-f-r-i-d-g-e."

Tabby rolled her eyes at me again. "Here, genius."

She had loaded the Apple mail app onto my phone. I felt damn stupid. I tapped into the correct section in my email client and wrote a general email asking from help with a devil baby and left my phone number. I could only hope that they would let it go through and I would get some aid for once. At least I was on the track of something again, instead of wallowing in my own thoughts.

I rubbed my temples. "Don't know why I didn't think of that sooner."

"Because you are technologically challenged." Tabby took the clothes from Woody and put them back in the shopping bags.

My phone rang. The caller ID displayed only a number. "Hello?"

"Mr. Holiday. My name is Father Shannon. How may I help you?"

I exhaled. "Thank God you've called. Things are such a mess."

"How so?"

"I believe the Order has been compromised. I've got a devil baby on my lap and I need a stiff drink."

The priest coughed. "I think you'd better start at the beginning."

"I was assigned Father Martin…"

I have no idea how long it took me to explain everything, but after I'd let it all out, I was drained. I guess that was how confessions were supposed to go, but it felt weird giving one when I hadn't done anything wrong.

"Is the child vicious?" he asked.

"No. He's sitting in my lap right now. He's pretty calm for a baby."

"That's a plus. Do not contact Father Martin for any reason. We will be sending help soon."

"Will you text me when?"

"No. Be prepared for us to come. We need you ready."

He hung up. Dread consumed me. But we couldn't escape with a devil baby in tow. And now, I was letting everything ride on a complete unknown. I truly was an idiot.

"What are you thinking about?" Tabby asked.

Something started taking form in my brain. Might be a protection we hadn't thought considered. That was, if we could control it.

"You have the weirdest expression on your face," she said.

I bit down on my cheek, then spat out, "Do you think we can weaponize Lucy?"

Woody cleared her throat. "Mr. Holiday, that is very dark magic you are speaking of."

I shrugged. "What difference does it make? We obviously killed someone."

"We killed a person who was trying to kill you. Weaponizing Lucy against those who could be immoral would be very, very bad."

She had a point. I was letting my imagination go again without taking the consequences into account. "They are coming. Don't know when, but that's what we got."

Woody nodded. "We will prepare. Be ready for war."

"I'm sorry, Jimmy," Tabby said. "But it was a dumb suggestion."

I shook my head. "It's okay, and I know. Our situation is impossible right now anyway. We still don't know who is coming. It might even end up okay."

Isaac meowed over my shoulder. I spun around to find Doc.

He took off his hat and stared at me. "What in tarnation have you got yourself into now?"

"The biggest mess in the world." At least, right now anyway. If the past year was any indication, I got in a lot of big messes. Most of them my own doing.

He tossed his hat onto the coffee table. "Why am I not surprised?"

"I've never been more happy to see a ghost in my life." Tabby beamed.

It tasted like I'd sucked a lemon. I kept thinking about myself and not worrying about the stress she was under. I needed to stop being such a dick.

"Calm your horses," Doc said. "I still got play in these old bones."

"Thank God for that." Hope bloomed for a change.

FOURTEEN
STRANGER IN A STRANGE LAND

AFTER WE GOT Doc caught up, I took a deep breath. It was nice to have things sort of like normal. Did I miss Lucy? Sure. But that was an issue I wasn't ready to address yet.

"So where have you been?" Tabby asked Doc.

"All over. Recharged. Talked to Lucy's father and explained things as best I could."

Tabby sighed. "I wish I could help him."

I slumped on the sofa. "I know it had to have been hard, but I appreciate you taking care of it. Talking to Will was on my list of things to address once things calmed down here."

Doc nodded. "It was my pleasure. He's a lost man, but I think he'll be okay."

"That's good," I said. "Any ideas about this one?" I tickled Ezekiel on my knee. He squealed good naturedly.

"Lots, but no things we should talk about now."

His eyes seemed darker than they had been before. I didn't like the cryptic vibe, but knowing Doc as I did, he had his reasons. I wanted things taken care of as soon as possible. I knew I couldn't sustain this level of stress much longer. Caring for a demon was turning out to be more trouble than exorcizing one.

Having Doc here again put me at ease with all of the

unknowns ahead. Had I known he was coming, I would have waited on decisions, but I had thought I'd never see him again after Lucy. I needed a damn psychic on my team.

"I will make one observation," Doc said, looking at me.

"I'll take any help I can get. What do you got for me?"

He cleared his throat. "You trust a devil baby more than Lucy."

I took a deep breath. He was right. Even though I'd had the vision, I still kept Ezekiel pretty much as he was. And when I thought of Lucy, I got a sour taste in my mouth. "At least Ezekiel hasn't tried to kill me."

Doc grunted. "Not yet."

I sighed. "You think I should let her loose?"

"I do."

It felt like the whole lot of them were ganging up on me and I didn't like it. I turned to Tabby. "Your thoughts on this?"

She stared at me. "It isn't fun, but life isn't fun. We can't watch either of them twenty-four hours a day. I think we should either let Lucy free at least part of every day or start locking Ezekiel up at night. It would be better to do what is fair."

I stood up. "And where would we lock him up? We can't put him in the same circle with Lucy. They will kill each other."

"Calm down. You don't know that."

I rolled my eyes. "Lucy knows nothing about taking care of a baby. And her new inclinations...I don't feel real comfortable."

Tabby raised her eyebrow at me. "You said."

I was losing points and I knew it. I scratched my head and turned to Woody. "Can we do a circle over here?"

Woody glanced at me from the corner of her eye. "Do I even have to answer that?"

I closed my eyes and counted to ten. Once I opened them, I took a deep breath. "I meant, do you mind putting one out here so she can interact?"

Woody grumbled. "I like to keep spell work where it belongs."

Tabby gave Woody the puppy dog eyes.

Woody readjusted herself in her chair. "You kids are going to be the death of me."

Once again, Lucy was freed of her box, and surrounded by a protective circle in the living room. In a way, I could understand Tabby's point. But Lucy had tried to kill me, not her. Ezekiel had bitten her, so I guess it was an okay trade. At least the one bite was just a nip early on and not the thing I had seen in my vision. I hoped she knew what she was doing.

I made it a point to stay out of the living room. I didn't feel like dealing with Lucy at all, and I wasn't going to be getting a lot of sleep since the chair I had been sleeping in was in the living room. Maybe I would go nap in the car.

"Jimmy, you can't keep this up," Tabby said.

I shook myself out of my daze. "Which thing can I not keep up? The devil baby, the killer ghost in the living room, or my own intense desire to self-destruct?"

Tabby smacked me. "Don't be a smart ass. That little girl in there loves you."

I nodded. Let the brainwashing commence. Nothing doing. I was not about to trust any of this shit anymore. "Sure she does. Maybe what she was before did, but this?" I motioned toward the living room. "This is not the Lucy I know."

Tabby sighed. "How do you think her parents felt?"

I threw up my hands, thankful that Ezekiel seemed content to sit at my feet for now. "Okay. How's this? I know it's fucked up that I'm trying to take care of this kid, and I know in my heart he's evil. But I also made a promise. Until I get some real help with him, I'm stuck."

Tabby grunted. "You are only stuck because you want to be."

"Jesus Christ, Tabby. Why are you busting my balls? I don't

care about Lucy anymore, got it? She's dead to me. I'll keep her soul safe until it's claimed, but that's it, and that's precisely what I should have done in the first place. And you should know the difference." She'd done it. She'd royally pissed me off. I wasn't sure if we could recover. I didn't think we could be together anymore. I'd had it. Friends maybe. But not like this. I had to know I could trust the person watching my back. And the fact that she was siding with the thing that tried to kill me kind of eliminated that trust factor.

She opened and closed her mouth several times like a fish, and then slapped me so hard across the face that my head whipped to the side. Then, she stormed out of the room.

"Fuck you!"

Isaac took one look at me and farted.

Ezekiel threw up all over my shoes.

All I wanted to do was go home.

I got myself and Ezekiel cleaned up. I did nod at Lucy as I passed, but there was no doubt about the coldness between us. She'd overheard the entire diatribe. Not that I was trying to hide anything, but the whole mess had irrevocably changed things. I was not about to be pushed into a corner. And if one more thing happened, I would leave them all there to fend for themselves.

I knew that eventually, something would need to be worked out, but to what extent and how? Who knew. Right now, we all needed to work together just enough to get Ezekiel some place safe. We didn't need to be best buddies to do that.

Suddenly, my phone rang. I answered it without thinking.

"Hello?"

"Mr. Holiday, how are things going? I've been expecting a report."

Mother fuck. It was Father Martin. I'd had enough of him too. "Like a shit storm. Exactly like I expected."

"Ah, so the event is not taken care of then?"

He was such a pompous ass wipe. "Not yet. I'm not exactly an expert—you know that. I'll turn in my report when I'm done."

"You do that."

When he hung up, I threw my phone on the table. "Asshole."

Woody came in and put a cookie in my free hand. "You eat that. I think your blood sugar is low. You've been grumpier than usual."

I laughed and shoved the cookie in my mouth. At least one person in the house didn't hate my guts.

Woody took Ezekiel from me and sat at the table. "You are going to have to work things out with her before big stuff starts."

I rolled my eyes. "I thought we already had the big stuff?"

Woody shook her head. "If I knew that witch at all, there are more than curses up in that house. That means the badness is just beginning."

I knew on some level she was right. And Martin's call was all too convenient. Him calling meant that either someone at the Order had tipped him off or he had a tracker on my email. Maybe both. I probably would never know for sure. "I can honestly say this is the first time he's called me in the middle of a case to ask how it is going."

Woody exhaled slowly. "When you get yourself wrapped up in something, you sure do it good."

I laughed. "It's one of my greatest talents."

Woody rubbed Ezekiel's back. The little guy's eyes started to slip closed. Then, she stared at me. "Get in there and fix this. We don't have the time or energy for it."

I wasn't about to argue. Tabby and I did need to work together, whether we liked it or not. There was no choice to make. Besides, I wasn't about to argue with Woody. She was my last true ally in this mess. "Yes, ma'am."

I walked into the one place I didn't want to go—the living room. Tabby was sitting in Woody's chair, staring out the window. I cleared my throat.

Tabby turned her head and glared at me.

I suppressed the urge to flip her off. "I think we were both shits a little bit ago. Nothing about this is easy, but more crap is coming and it would be better to push all this aside until we get out of danger."

She jerked up. "What danger?"

I rubbed my temples. "Father Martin called wanting to know why I haven't provided an update yet."

"Sounds like you've been compromised."

"We all have. That is, if you continue to hang around me. And there seems to be more to it. Woody thinks there's something left for us up in that house."

Tabby's eyes narrowed. "Why does she think that?"

"I don't know. She didn't say." I didn't question it either. Woody knew.

"I could go find out what it is," Lucy said quietly.

I turned around and stared at her. "While that's a noble suggestion, I'm not sure it's a good idea. There's no telling how far those curses will go."

And I worried about letting her loose. Screwing up those curses would mess up Tabby too. That wasn't the issue. Lucy hadn't even tried to do anything to harm Tabby, let alone touch her. If Lucy went up there, then inadvertently brought the curse back with her, it could kill us all.

"To be honest, we need a drone or something to look around the house," Tabby said.

I snorted. "God, I wish. But nowhere to get anything like that. And I doubt I have access to those fancy credit cards anymore."

"Wait a minute." Tabby stood up. "Wouldn't the curses already be breached?"

I scratched my head. "What do you mean?"

She pointed toward the witch's house. "Those guys already went up there to collect all the bodies of the priests. The one's that had stopped by around the time of your vision. So people were already inside the house."

I peered through the window. The house seemed quiet. There was only one thing up there that did not belong. An extra vehicle. "The car is still up there."

"Let me out so I can see," Lucy said.

No use anymore. The constant questioning my reasoning and attacks against my thoughts were taking their toll. I inclined my head at Tabby. "If she kills me, it's on you."

I didn't wait for an answer. I walked to the protective circle and dragged my foot through the salt. The circle was broken. Lucy was free.

She stepped outside of the circle and stood next to me.

I looked down at her. "You go up there and see what you can see. Don't go in the house. See if you can find out what happened to the priests."

"I'll be back," she said, then disappeared.

"I'm proud of you," Tabby said.

I shook my head. I didn't give a damn what she thought. I'd caved. If it all turned into one giant mess, it was her fault. I was done being a lap dog. "I'm either a genius or goddamned stupid."

"It's not good to take the Lord's name in vain, especially now," Woody said from the peanut gallery.

I wanted to say so many things, but I bit my tongue until it bled.

"She has a point," Tabby said.

I sighed and eyed the room. My ancestor hadn't been around in a while. "Where's Doc?"

Tabby shrugged. "Dunno. Haven't seen him."

I closed my eyes. Now was not the time to get myself all worked up. It was comforting having him around, but not a necessity. "Okay. Let's prepare not to have him. We don't know when all this shit is going to go down. We better be ready."

"Sounds good to me."

Turns out, we didn't have too much to do. Wasn't like we had an arsenal of weapons. We had next to nothing to work with—at least from my perspective. We had Tabby's and Woody's spells, a chicken foot, my voice, and one devil baby. Our odds sucked. I didn't bother to pray because I didn't even know what to pray for.

We went through the motions with meals. Even Ezekiel seemed nervous. His eyes kept flitting toward the door. He didn't take a nap.

Finally, Lucy appeared in the kitchen.

I almost fell to the floor, I was so relieved. Much more stress and I was going to drop dead of a stroke.

"Thank God you're back," Tabby said.

Lucy nodded. "It's bad."

"Like how bad?" I asked. No sense in dwelling on the crap I could do nothing about. Lucy's information might help.

She glanced up at me. "Remember that movie with the people that changed into demons in the theatre. The cheesy one with the funny music?"

My brain rolled through a number of movies, but it seemed like about ten fit that description. "Vaguely."

"That's what's up there."

I blinked. "Demons?"

She nodded. "All those men have big pointy teeth and milky eyes."

Leave it to Lucy to describe creatures from an old Italian horror film. I needed a drink. Junk food was not going to cut it. I needed more. "Okay. That's not good. Any chance they could come this way?"

"They're heading here now."

I whipped my head around. "Got anything to fight demons, Woody?"

She sighed and flitted around the kitchen. "Sure do. Get me some holy water, Mr. Holiday. It's time you saw truly what God can do."

I grabbed a pitcher from the sink and filled it with water. This was going to be quick and dirty, but it couldn't be helped. I took a deep breath and let loose my Marker voice with my hand in the water. "God help me. Bless this water. Help us fight the unholy. Help us make things right. Bless this water in the name of the Father, the Son, and the Holy Ghost. Amen."

A slight oil slick seemed to fan over the water for a minute before it disappeared. At least I did that right. "All right, Woody. It's ready."

Woody set Ezekiel on the floor, then leaned over and patted his head. "Be good and stay here in the house. Bad things out there."

Ezekiel whined and reached for me. His lips were quivering like he was about to cry. I crouched down. "I know, bud. It's scary. Promise me, if any of those things come in here, protect the kitty."

He nodded.

With as much as Ezekiel liked Isaac, it wasn't a bad thought. Hopefully, we could keep anything from getting that close, but it also made him feel like he was doing something without him getting into direct danger. I stood back up. "Let's kick some demon ass."

"You are so droll." Tabby smiled.

We stepped onto the porch in an old fashioned Mexican standoff. I didn't take the time to ponder Tabby's happiness. Between the fights and the mood swings, I was lost. The demons, all seven of them, were snarling and staring at us.

Green drool poured from their mouths in strings. When it hit the grass, it sizzled. I kept expecting one of them to pause and start trying to summon their dark lord, but nothing that cliché happened. Their teeth were large and misplaced in their mouths. Almost as if they needed major dental work. At first, I thought we were all standing there until something worse showed up. The seconds seemed to tick by so slowly, as if they were really minutes. And then one leapt and it was on.

I barely got the cup in my hand and had thrown before it hit the porch. It splashed the creature in the face and it screamed. Pustules formed on its face and pulsated then finally burst with milky red sludge.

It was like a show, throwing water from cups and it landing on top of the demons.

Once the first had gotten injured the rest had rushed the porch. All three of us kept grabbing cups of water and flinging them, most of the time not even paying attention where we were throwing it. I'm sure it was ridiculous.

The creatures screamed and bubbled some more. Their heads were masses of oozing flesh, yet still they tried to press forward. When I ran out of water, I moved behind the others. I watched their pitchers start to get low too. This wasn't working out the way I had hoped. I closed my eyes and raised my voice, "You do not belong here. I damn you back to Hell!"

The power rippled from me, but the creatures didn't even pause. They kept moving forward. "Fuck!"

One was staggering up the steps of the porch, getting a little too close. Even the water wasn't phasing it now.

Woody stopped throwing water and raised her hands high above her head. "God of light. God of love. Hear us now. Send these foul beings back into the dark where they belong."

Thunder burst forth through the sky.

A bolt of lightning struck the demon climbing up the porch. Its head exploded and its hands blew off. The body tumbled into the grass. Where each body stood, a lightning strike hit. The demons didn't even have time to run away from them. The electricity crackled through the air and it all smelled of burning meat. Once the strikes stopped, each body was a scorch mark in the grass. The bodies had become some sort of black sludge in the grass. As soon as all the demons were gone, the storm stopped as quickly as it had started.

Woody turned to me. "You see, there are times to use magic and there are times to ask God for help."

Back in the house, I was trying to figure out how to pull myself together. My hands kept shaking. I had been lulled into a false sense of security that my power could solve anything, but I'd been wrong. I could have gotten us killed if it hadn't been for Woody. I'd let my own pride get in the way.

It was dark now, which made my stomach clench. And although I knew that there wasn't much left to lurk in the dark, I was still scared. I was back to how things were before I even knew I was a Marker. I felt so damn vulnerable.

Tires spun on the gravel out front. I peered through the kitchen window. I watched as a guy grabbed something out of his car, threw a newspaper over his head, and ran up the steps. I met him at the door.

"Mr. Holiday?"

I scanned his body with my eyes. Nothing seemed out of the ordinary. "Yes."

He cocked his head to the side, as if wanting to gain entrance. "I'm Father Shannon. May I come in for a talk?"

I glanced over my shoulder. I did not see Tabby or Lucy.

Woody nodded at me from her place near the refrigerator. I opened the door wide enough for him to enter. The father squeezed past me and took off his shoes inside the door.

"Where is a good place to talk?" he asked.

Woody opened the door to the fridge and started rummaging. "Go on into the living room with Jimmy. I'll put on some coffee."

I nodded to her and led the Father into the living room. Tabby was sitting on the couch, her hair balled up on the top of her head. Lucy and Ezekiel were on the floor, watching Isaac chase a string he had found. This was the closest I had seen Ezekiel to Isaac. Lucy must have either calmed Isaac down or he was so happy to have his playmate back, he was too distracted to be worried about Ezekiel.

Father Shannon froze as soon as his eyes landed on Ezekiel.

"You weren't kidding," he said.

I chuckled. "Nope. I never do about things like this."

He stared at me. "Can he talk?"

"No, too young." I walked over and picked up Ezekiel. He cooed as he wrapped his tail around my waist.

The Father's hands shook. He motioned to Tabby. "May I sit down?"

She patted the couch cushion beside her.

Father Shannon took a moment to regain his composure, then he smiled at Ezekiel. "What's happened to the baby's mother?"

I rubbed Ezekiel's back. He started to purr.

"That's a long story I'm not sure you want to hear," I said.

Woody came in and set coffee cups in front of Tabby and the Father. Then, she went and sat in her chair. I was content holding my little buddy. Felt safer for him. At least if Father Shannon tried any nonsense, I could run.

"How long have you worked for this organization?" Woody asked him.

He took a sip of his coffee. "Not long. Only a couple of months."

"And how experienced are you with the inner workings?" I wanted to know how far into this he was. And more importantly, if he was one of Martin's goons.

He swallowed hard. "Not very well. I was given email duty. Since you said you had problems, I didn't want to talk to anyone."

I sighed. I could tell he wasn't lying. Not about his job anyway. There was something about his eyes though. Something I couldn't nail down. "That was probably a good idea, but I'm not so sure how much it will help. You might be in very great danger and I might have put you there."

"What are you going to do with him?" Shannon pointed at Ezekiel.

That was the question. At least I hadn't needed to explain everything to the upmost extent with this guy. A plus. "He's a mystery right now. His mother is dead. The Order member who sent me to find him seems out to sabotage me, and anytime I try the church, something bad happens to the priests."

His eyes grew wide. "Seriously?"

"You have no idea," Tabby said, searching her coffee cup.

I walked over next to the Father. "If you know of a safe place to take Ezekiel, I'm all for it. But apart from that, I truly don't know what to do."

Father Shannon gulped. "I know where to take him. But it isn't pretty."

I stared at him. That was the most honest thing I had heard in days. Finally, someone I could trust. "I don't care what it is as long as he will be safe and unhurt."

The Father took a sip of his coffee. "There is this place..."

Tabby sat up straighter on the sofa. "What type of place?"

He set his cup on Woody's table. "I overheard some of the others talking about it a few weeks ago. An old monastery in Eastern Europe. Things that can't be controlled or contained are kept there."

"And you're sure they could handle Ezekiel?" I didn't even know what all he was capable of.

He nodded. "Like I said, it won't be pretty. He will be in a cage most likely, but he will be safe from harming himself and other people."

"And why should we trust you?" Woody asked. She was leaning forward in her chair, almost like a cat about to pounce.

He glanced over at her. "I don't think you have too many choices. And I can't even promise that I can give updates on him or anything. That might be for the best. But you certainly can't keep him. Too many people will be after him."

"What is it that he can do?" I asked.

Shannon leaned into the sofa. "From the archives I was able to access, most of these children don't display the markings. They have certain abilities, but they do not look like he does."

While interesting, I wasn't sure what it meant for our situation. "And that's important why?"

He stared at me thoughtfully for a moment. "Because he wasn't made by a lesser demon. In fact, I would say he was made by the Devil himself."

You could hear a pin drop in the room. I had thought about it before, but had shelved it in the back of my mind as impossible. Once again, here was proof I had some sort of connection to Big Red. My body shivered. I almost expected my breath to blow out in a cloud, but it didn't. Ezekiel squirmed to look at Isaac. Isaac chirped and rubbed against my legs before going on his merry way.

"When can you take him?" Tabby asked.

"The sooner the better."

I walked across the room and handed Ezekiel to Woody. Then, I turned to stare at the good Father. "Will you let me do something to satisfy my curiosity?"

He shrugged. "I suppose so, as long as it will not harm me."

I straightened my back and pushed out power. I knew this part of my power still worked. And I wasn't about to risk giving

Ezekiel over to someone without making sure they weren't possessed. "Name yourself. In the power of Earth, Air, Fire, and Water, reveal yourself to me!"

The Father rose from the sofa. "I am Father Thomas Shannon and I've been alive for a very long time. I am not, nor have I ever been, part of the demonic faction."

I paused. Where in the world were all of these immortals or really old people coming from? It was enough to make my head hurt. "What are you talking about?"

"I am not as young as I look. There is a reason for that, but it has no bearing on us at the moment. I only joined the Order a few months ago. But I graduated seminary in nineteen-thirty-four."

He didn't look older than his twenties.

Tabby choked. "What are you?"

"Unfortunately, immortal. God gave me the gift. What I am is never documented publicly. That would require science to expand their beliefs. I spend my time investigating around the church and helping God keep evil at bay."

"And you know of this monastery by others' conversations?" I asked. Him being immortal or not wasn't the concern. I needed to know if I could trust him.

"Yes, though they are listed in the archives. I've never needed them until now. Never thought about them to be honest. I'm immortal, not God-like."

I chuckled. I was liking this guy. His way of giving answers to my fears was calming me down. "And you are willing to risk your life for Ezekiel?"

"Is that his name?"

I nodded.

He took a deep breath and sat on the sofa again. "I can promise I will do everything I can to get him to the monastery. I am not easy to kill, but it is not impossible. I cannot control things out of my control."

Part of me didn't want Ezekiel out of my sight, but with

Father Martin breathing down my neck, Ezekiel needed to get out of here—and fast. I had no other options anymore. If I planned on keeping Ezekiel away from Martin, it was the best choice. "Okay. Take him. Make him safe."

Father Shannon nodded, got up from the couch, walked over to Woody, and gently took Ezekiel from her.

Tabby hopped up. "Wait here."

The Father paused and tickled Ezekiel. Ezekiel giggled.

That was it then. If Ezekiel didn't sense anything bad, it was going to be okay. He warned us against his mother after all. The kid had killer spidey senses.

Tabby handed Father Shannon the shopping bags full of baby stuff. "All of this should help."

Father Shannon took them in one hand while keeping Ezekiel steady with the other. He nodded and smiled at Tabby. Woody got up and put her arms around me. Tabby followed the Father out of the room. Woody didn't let go until we could no longer hear the tires on the gravel. I guess she knew me better than I thought she did. Would I have tried to take him back? Probably. I had gotten used to the little dude. Likely the only kid I would ever have—only living one anyway.

I swallowed hard and forced myself to calm down. I'd done the best thing I could. I'd kept my promise. Ezekiel was safe. "You can let go now. I'm all right."

Tabby came back in and approached me cautiously. "It's going to be okay."

I stared at her. Part of me couldn't believe she'd said that. The other part had no trouble realizing it. "No, it isn't. But nothing is okay these days. Now, I gotta focus, deal with Martin, and wait for real hell to reign down."

"Unless the Order steps in."

I almost fell to me knees I laughed so hard. Finally, once I composed myself enough, I stared at her. "Wishful thinking?"

Her eyes were a little watery. "Yeah."

FIFTEEN
A BEAUTIFUL LIE

SLEEP THAT NIGHT WAS FITFUL. Every time I heard the house crack or settle, I jerked awake. Nothing was going to make me relax. And as much as I didn't want to admit it, I needed to feel like someone had faith in me. With Tabby and everything that had happened, faith was something that no longer existed where I was concerned. Faith in God? That was a whole other issue.

Long about three, I heard my phone vibrate. I pulled it from my pocket and took a peek. I had a text message from an unknown number. I tapped on it. All it said was, "He is safe."

I took a deep breath and stared off into the darkness of the room. At least I had done something right. Whether it was worth it still remained to be seen.

I rubbed my eyes, thankful the others were asleep. Seeing me like this only served to make them think I was weaker than they already thought. Lucy crept over and hugged me. I let her.

The next morning, the sun was shining and birds were chirping from somewhere I couldn't see. It was so damn cliché. I wasn't about to believe it was a sign. I'd seen too many horrible things on beautiful days.

I sat there for a moment, listening to the workings happening in the kitchen. From the sound of it, Tabby and Woody had long been up. Doc was sitting on the floor, playing with Lucy.

"Where have you been?" I asked him. I could have used his advice and his backup.

He grunted. "Keeping an eye on things."

Figuring that was about all I was going to get, I hauled my ass off the chair and walked into the kitchen. From the looks of things, Tabby had just finished helping Woody do all the dishes and set things to rights. "Plans for the day?" I figured I might be a good idea to ask. My involvement was lessened quite a bit since the devil baby issue was no more.

"We need to look at that house," Woody said as she plopped her dish cloth over the faucet.

"And as much as you don't want to, you need to turn in your report," Tabby replied. She was leaning with her back against the counter. Her hair seemed like fire in the sunlight. Shades of red undulated as she breathed.

I shook myself. Would do me no good to get lost in her again. Things had gone sour and it was best I not forget that. I sunk into the chair. "Which one should we do first?"

"Let's go check out that house." Woody glanced through the window, then turned around to face me.

"All right."

It was weird going up there without having things pop out from any direction. I'd been so used to having all manner of insanity happen, the calm was a serious shock to my system.

Lucy and Doc stayed at Woody's house with Isaac. At least that way we could ensure they wouldn't get caught in some left-over spirit trap. I wouldn't put anything by that bitch of a witch.

The house was more weather beaten now, either because I knew someone lived there before or there was a heck of a glamor on it. Either one was possible. Though, I did wonder why that woman would have cared what her house looked like, unless it was simply for my benefit.

Woody crept up the porch first. She had the most experience with this type of magic after all. Up against most of the crap we'd encountered lately, I would be cannon fodder if I stood up to it. Woody could fight back.

Minus the paint that was peeling more than I remembered, everything was relatively the same, except for the blood stains left behind from what had happened. Woody mumbled something under her breath, then opened the door. Tabby and I followed her into the house. The scent of rot and decay slammed me in the face. I tried not to gag. It was so bad it smelled like the house had been used to butcher cattle and then left in hundred-degree heat.

"What smells so bad?" Tabby asked, holding her hand over her nose.

I shook my head. "No idea. The dead were in the yard. Could be residual fluids from the one that was in there a while."

"If that's the case, how could Ezekiel's mother stand it?" Tabby asked.

Woody scanned the walls and kept changing directions. "We have no idea what she was used to."

"I'm really happy that bodies killed supernaturally seem to disappear." That is, except for Lucy's body, but that was something else entirely. I was glad that skin suit never came back for me. I still had nightmares about the damn thing.

"In here," she said, darting into a side room.

Tabby and I followed her and entered what I guessed was a

sitting room. The old mantelpiece over the fireplace was covered in grime. Thick soot stretched from the fireplace up the wall.

"Right there." Woody pointed at the wall opposite the fireplace.

I followed her finger. Above our heads, in large letters, written in blood was, "She is coming."

"What the fuck does that mean?" I asked.

Woody grunted. "It means we're going to have more trouble than your report. Let's get out of here and sure up the wards around the house. If I'm right, we're going to need them."

Tabby's eyes went as wide as saucers. We hurried out of the house with Woody and went back down the hill. Once inside, Woody started grabbing herbs from cupboards. She didn't even slow down long enough to take a breath. "Tabby help me with this. Jimmy, get that broom and sweep all the dirt off the floor of this house and get it outside."

I didn't question her reasoning. I grabbed the broom she pointed to and got to work. It wasn't like there was any dirt to see, but I knew better. I swept the floor of every room— including the spellroom. I even moved the furniture I could move by myself. When I was done, I swept the meager collectings outside. I knew it was impossible to get every microscopic piece, but I hoped I had done okay.

"Off the porch too?" I asked Woody, sticking my head into the door.

"Yes." She nodded. "Thank you."

I got it all off the porch and the steps. Even rubbed the broom in the grass to try to eliminate as much dust as possible, then I went back inside the house.

"Good."

She snatched the broom from my hand.

"Now, stay out of my way. Go sit down." She went outside and closed the door behind her.

My stomach clenched into knots tighter than ever. That was the tersest Woody had ever spoken to me. And if she was that flustered, it didn't bode well. I spied Doc and Lucy peering at me from the archway. I motioned for them to follow me and we arranged ourselves in the living room to be as much out of the way as possible.

I didn't see Tabby anywhere. Woody probably had her doing more.

"If it's bad, can I fight?" Lucy asked, suddenly. Her eyes pleaded with me.

I stared at her. "You know if I say yes, Tabby will kill me. But I put it this way. If you and Doc are in danger, save yourselves. Don't do it for us. Only try if you have no other choice."

Doc patted Lucy's head. "Don't be trying to save me either. I've been around for a long time. If I need to go, so be it. Save yourself."

Lucy pouted. "I don't know if I can do that."

I sighed. "You have to promise me you'll try really hard. And if you must, save Tabby. I've been down the shit hole too much. With what happened between us, I wouldn't expect you to save me, so don't."

Lucy's eyes welled with tears.

I reached toward her. "Don't cry. Stuff got messed up on so many levels. Please, don't cry over me."

Doc rolled his eyes. "You really are horrible with children."

I chuckled sadly. "I know."

Tabby collapsed beside me on the sofa. "I haven't been this tired since I moved."

I guessed our disagreements didn't matter anymore since we were both likely not to make it out of this whole thing alive. That was what my gut was telling me anyway. "I don't doubt it. I don't know how you do what you do. My stuff is all this voice. I don't have anything else. You have to do the whole gamut. Thanks for helping Woody."

Tabby nodded and stretched. "I don't think she's as strong as she'd like us to believe she is. Not magically, physically I mean."

Now that she'd mentioned it, Woody didn't seem as bubbly as she had been a few days ago. Of course, battling zombies, demons, and evil witches would take energy out of anybody, and Woody actually fought them. I mostly watched. "We've probably been the most excitement she's seen in years, and I don't mean that in a good way."

Tabby got up and peeked through the picture window. "She will be done soon, then you and I can figure out lunch. We need food."

"Yeah. Okay. No problem. Let me know."

Tabby went back into the kitchen.

"This ain't lookin' good, Jimmy," Doc said, stepping from the shadows of the hallway.

I sighed. I truly wished my gut was wrong. I nodded to him. "I know." I got up off the couch and walked into the kitchen. Doc did not follow.

Woody stopped in front of me after she closed the door to the porch. She seemed so tired, I almost expected her to fall down. She stared at me for a moment and seemed to pull strength from somewhere. "We have some talking to do."

I held up my hand to try to stop her from going anywhere else. "Why don't you sit down while Tabby and I make lunch? You can tell us what you want to while we work."

Tabby nodded appreciatively behind Woody, and then she crossed the room and pulling things from the fridge.

"I don't know if we'll survive this," Woody said. She didn't seem mad, only matter of fact.

"Why? Who's coming?" Granted, I had the same feeling, but I wasn't about to say I knew everything. I needed to know how to fight whatever was coming.

Woody leaned forward toward me. "If I'm right, it is the dark witch that was in league with her the first time. DeRoche."

Woody didn't use names often when referring to the dark witches. I suspected it was the same as demons; you tried not to speak their names because names held power.

"And what about this woman scares you?" Tabby asked.

Woody seemed to fade away for a second, like her soul wasn't behind her eyes any longer. After a bit, she came back. "Now, bear in mind I have no idea who trained Mrs. Timberlake. But DeRoche knew much more than she did. A lot of their workings were things I hadn't even seen before. But that isn't the worst part."

"Okay. How can it get any worse?" I asked.

Woody winked at me. "Mrs. DeRoche isn't alive anymore. Her body was found in a flood way back when. But her ghost walked and continued causing trouble. She disappeared for a time when that first devil baby was taken away."

"How can you be so sure it's her that's coming?" Tabby asked.

"Because she's the only one that ever scared me. And the fact that we have already dispatched with Mrs. Timberlake."

I froze. Not something I wanted to hear or would make me feel all happy inside. The past and the present were merging in an odd way. This was so beyond my pay grade. "On another note, when should I send in my report?"

Tabby laughed at me. "What is your plan here?"

I grinned. "Since Father Martin has had some sort of agenda in place, I'm betting there is a good chance he's going to be pissed off. Might as well have it hit all at once. That way, we won't have to continuously search around every corner—that is if we survive this thing."

Tabby turned to Woody. "Jimmy thrives on chaos, if you can't tell."

Woody tapped her fingers on the table "Make your play. Maybe it will give us a little bit of an edge."

I took my phone into the living room and opened my email app.
I was glad Tabby had fixed this for me. Otherwise, I'd be calling
in the report, and I'd rather not talk to Father Martin if I could
keep from it. I'd already accidentally done it and I didn't relish
doing it again. I reminded myself to be more aware.

Father Martin,

The saga of the devil baby is now complete. Unfortunately, through the course of events beyond my control, the
mother died. I can confirm that the child was some sort of
mutant or hybrid between human and demon. He has been
remanded to a safe place where they are used to dealing with
creatures like him. I cannot tell you the exact location. I do
know it is in Europe somewhere. At any rate, no more
demon baby. No more problem for the Order.

I'll be awaiting my next assignment.
J. Holiday

As soon as I hit send, I floated on a cloud. I still didn't know
which way was up, but at least I'd kept my morals intact. That
accounted for something. I figured it would be best to wait to
announce my resignation until I got home, if I made it. That way
I would be on turf I trusted.

I walked back into the kitchen. "Now watch for the shot that
started the Civil War."

Tabby held her hand against her forehead. "Sit down and eat
something, will you?"

I alternated between her and Woody. "How long do we
have?"

Woody sighed. "There's no telling."

I wasn't surprised. Nothing to do with the supernatural

could be tied up all pretty with a bow. I wished Woody would have had some type of trick to know when the next hit was coming. But had I thought about it, if she'd known when bad crap was coming, she wouldn't have had to fight so much.

My phone started ringing. I stared at the screen. It was the man himself. "Here we go boys and girls."

I answered the phone. "Hello?"

"What do you mean the child is safe? The child was mine!"

I forced myself not to laugh at his ridiculous bad guy shit. "Beautiful afternoon to you too, Father. Yes, the baby is all safe and sound."

I could hear him grumble through the phone. After a minute or two of heavy breathing, he began again, "Is this some sort of revenge for misleading you? If that's all it is, I'm sorry. It won't happen again."

Jesus Christ. He was so slimy. I wished he'd shown this side of him sooner. "No. No joke."

He roared into the phone. I had to pull it away from my ear. "How could you be so stupid? This is not acceptable, Mr. Holiday. Not acceptable at all."

I steadied my anger. My patience had run dry. "I don't care what you think, Father Martin. I quit. You can have your money. I'm out." I was over the whole thing. Home turf or not, screw them. I would work fast food if I had to.

His voice turned then. "But Mr. Holiday, you can't quit. There is no quitting the Order."

I snorted. "What are you going to do to me, kill me? Really? I'm bound by God, not any organization."

He growled. "I'm warning you, Mr. Holiday. Repent and help us find the child. Everything will be forgiven."

I almost searched for a hidden camera somewhere. This was not coming across as scary. It was over the top and pointless, like I was on a reality show. "No dice. I won't sell my soul for a paycheck."

He grunted. "All right, then, Mr. Holiday. You've made your choice. We'll be in touch."

I tossed my phone onto the table and stared at Woody and Tabby. "Made another enemy."

Tabby sighed. "What else were you expecting?"

"Not sure, but it was the way he sounded, like some throwback from a horror movie. Kept ranting about me giving away 'his child'. Very weird." The term Satanist came to mind, except I knew for a fact there were completely normal people who were part of the Satanic religion. Normal in a broad sense, anyway. While I didn't agree with a lot of their teachings, they also were not performing human sacrifices in the basement, and that was the type Martin sounded like.

"Uh-huh," Woody said. "Are you sure this Order is really a thing?"

If it hadn't been for Shannon, I would wonder. Now, how big of an organization it was remained to be seen. Of course, Shannon could have been snowing me too. Anything was possible. "You know, it is certainly possible that anyone can give you email, technology, and money in your bank account if you give them your account information. All I'd known about them when I started was what had been put on an iPad and I'd been given my Mark."

"And the Mark didn't happen at the same time?" she asked.

"No. The Mark happened on my first case. I'd been helping a friend. It's how I got Lucy in the first place. It was almost two months later when the Order left their iPad in my house."

"That sounds like something not remotely connected to the church," Woody said.

I shrugged. "What does it sound like?"

She lowered her eyes to the table. "Nothing good."

If that was the case, then I had no idea. It certainly wasn't apparent in my cases. Of course, it could be how Big Red's eye landed on me in the first place. But ultimately, there were too many questions for me to consider Woody's idea as golden. "Are you telling me I've been working for Satanists? What about the Vatican Exorcism School?"

Woody shrugged. "No idea about that. Could be a few bad eggs."

"That sounds more likely," Tabby said. "Otherwise, I would think that Jimmy's exorcism wouldn't have worked after he teamed up with them. Plus, there was Father Shannon."

Woody nodded for a moment. "You have a point. Maybe I am getting paranoid in my old age. Let's try to get some rest. I suspect the attack will happen after dark."

SIXTEEN
THE KILL

IT WAS impossible to nap with everything hanging over my head, but it wasn't like that was Tabby's or Woody's problem. Maybe they were a lot more tired than me. They both snored softly while I sat wide awake. I did miss my bed, and that likely had something to do with it. Sleeping in a chair after a while wasn't the most fun thing in the world.

Whatever the reason, I gave up on sleep and tiptoed into the spellroom. Lucy and Doc followed. I hadn't asked them, but I appreciated their camaraderie.

"I never could sleep before a battle either," Doc said. "Too much chaos coming."

I nodded. "I think that's part of the problem. I also don't like how Woody has been put in danger because of our meddling. And some of her questions have left me uneasy."

Doc flashed a lopsided grin. "That woman isn't about to be dragged into anything. Besides, with the history between her and those witches, I think it's all been building for a while. And maybe God put her here to help since he knew you'd be clueless."

I laughed. "Thanks a lot."

Lucy stared at the floor. "I don't want you to die. I didn't even want you to die before. I only wanted you to feel what I felt."

I couched down and looked her in the eye. "Honey, you do realize that no one can bring me back from the dead, right? Once I'm dead, I'm gone."

She blinked. "Not unless you're like me."

I didn't know how to explain this or fix it. "But wouldn't you rather I stay where I can help you instead of having to go away and recharge like Doc does? Besides, I think if I die, you go away because your energy is tied to me. God would collect you and fight it out with the Devil."

She sighed. "I don't think so. I'm not important enough."

I had no way of making her feel better. I wished I could curl up in a pile of warm towels instead of face whatever we were going to have to face. "If you weren't important, then why would God have brought me to you in the first place? He could have let Asmodeus have you."

"He's right. God cares about every soul." Doc's eyes flashed toward the door. "We best get out there."

I didn't take the time to ask and darted from the room. I trusted Doc's sensors way better than my own. I rushed to the living room. Tabby and Woody were already up, staring at me.

"Doc thought he heard something," I said.

We all listened. When nothing came of it, Woody sat in her chair. "Guess we'll know shortly. We needed to get up anyway."

Tabby slumped onto the sofa. Her dark circles had dark circles of their own. "I feel like I could sleep for a thousand years."

I glanced at her. "You and me too, kiddo."

"Where are Doc and Lucy?" Tabby asked.

"Spellroom. Or at least that's where we were talking."

She nodded. "When we get home, I want a puppy."

I snorted. "And how do you think Isaac will like that?"

"He'll get used to it."

Tabby went into the bathroom. I found myself thinking of Ezekiel. I missed having him hold onto me. I even missed his snakey tail. But Doc was right, I sucked with kids.

Woody stood up. "Let's make us a feast. Might be a good idea to rally ourselves."

We emptied out not only the fridge, but the freezer too. Lasagna, homemade garlic bread, salad, roasted asparagus, tomatoes sliced with some olive oil, and a giant coconut cake for dessert filled the table. By the time we were done, I was surprised we could even move, we were so full.

While we enjoyed the food, a saddened pall had set in. We were quiet as we ate. Granted, we shoveled it in, but I wasn't so sure any of us fully enjoyed it. After we were done, we put away the leftovers, but left the dishes in the sink. What did we care about dishes if this was our last evening alive? If we were still living tomorrow morning, we could take on the task then. Besides, Tabby and Woody figured having the extra garlic stinking up the kitchen might help. I wasn't sure how that would work, but they were the experts on that sort of thing, not I. There was very little I was an expert at.

We made sure the back door was locked and the extra wards set. Then, we all went back into the living room. I walked over to the picture window and glanced up the hill toward the witch's house.

"Holy shit."

"What?" Tabby asked and came over.

I pointed.

Instead of the abandoned black gaping windowed form I'd expected, all the windows of the house glowed with this eerie neon green light. The house still appeared abandoned, but with the green light coming from it, it was all damn strange. As we were watching, the light seemed to be slowly moving upward. A great cracking sound boomed and the house bent and buckled, folding in on itself over and over until all that was left was that green light. The house had been swallowed up by some supernatural force.

"I think that's our cue," Tabby said.

I twitched. "I think we should have run."

"Wouldn't have worked," Woody said, coming up behind me. "They follow—as you know."

I sighed. "Could have bought us some time."

"For what?"

I didn't answer. She was right. I wanted to avoid this like nothing else, but it was a cancer eating away at who we were. The longer we put it off, the worse it was going to get. And what had happened to us mentally had already been pretty fucking bad.

"You okay?" Tabby asked me.

I glanced at her. "I guess so. Doesn't matter anyway. Still going to happen."

"I love you."

It felt so good to hear her say it. All of the pain and bullshit from the last few days didn't matter anymore. I dragged her into my arms and hugged her. "If we make it through this, we're going to Vegas. We can have an official ceremony later."

Tabby laughed. "You are insufferable."

"Probably."

Right when I was about to relax, the house started to shake so bad, it felt like it would slide off its foundation.

"Are we ever going to stop having crap like this happen?" Tabby asked.

"I don't know."

The house shook again. I thought about ducking under the table, but I wasn't sure that would provide all that much protection.

"What do we do?" I asked Woody.

She examined the cracked corners in the kitchen. "Nothing right now. Let her use up some of that power. We don't leave this place until she breaks the wards. Until then we stay where we are."

I'd never fought a fight like this in my life. I was used to fighting demons, not witches. This was way beyond even Tabby's scope of expertise. We were out of our element. Tabby was the type of witch that helped people with things. Battle magic was not something she'd ever been trained in—not that she wouldn't have loved to learn. I knew her too well.

The house shook again. This time, I heard something snap, almost as if the ceiling buckled, but I saw no evidence of it. "I don't like the sound of that."

"Not yet," Woody said.

Doc and Lucy appeared in the living room with us. Lucy shook.

"Is she going to tear down the house?" Tabby asked.

"Maybe," Woody replied.

"Come out here," a voice said from outside. It was strong, feminine, and sure of itself.

"We aren't coming out there until you make us," Woody said.

We heard a cackle from outside that seemed to dance along the perimeter of the house. It was strange and I knew anyone normal would assume it was an auditory hallucination.

"Should we pray?" I asked.

Woody shook her head. "Not yet. We have to save that for when it will hit her worst. She's wily and will only give us one shot."

The house rumbled again. I heard glass break somewhere in the house, but I couldn't pinpoint the source. It was not in the kitchen, and it sounded more like a window versus something small.

"I don't like this," Lucy said.

"I'm not crazy about it much either," I replied.

"Lulu, I'm not going to stay out here all night. I will come in there and get you if I have to," the voice said.

Woody stepped closer to the door. "Nothing doing. You think

we're that ignorant? I'm that stupid? It might be a few years since I've seen you, but I wasn't born yesterday."

I heard some metal crunch.

"I hope that wasn't the car," Tabby said.

I prayed it wasn't the car. Without it, we'd have no way to get back home. "You and me both. I'd hate to try to explain that to the insurance company."

Another crunch and the loud sound of a car horn blasted. I held my head in my hands. "Shit."

After a minute, the horn squealed and died.

"I don't even want to look at that," Tabby said.

"Me either."

"I'm running out of things to play with," the voice said.

"I know you!" Woody stepped so close to the door she was touching it. "You like to play with illusion. And you like to lie. Did you finally get someone to give you a body?"

My eyes darted to Tabby. She glanced back at me wide-eyed.

"Nobody gives me anything," the voice said. "I made this. Better than yours anyway."

I crept closer behind Woody and peered through the little window over the counter next to the door. More of the green glow was there, and faintly standing near the bushes was something out of a nightmare. It was part mannequin and part metal. Springs were drilled into the mannequin parts in various places. Some seemed to have bits of wire connecting bits of the monstrosity together. Others seemed to be there for decoration. It was half robot and half monster.

"Want me to egg it on?" I asked Woody quietly.

"Are you out of your ever loving mind? Shut up and get back," she hissed.

I backed away. It was the ugliest thing I had ever seen. It looked like the girl from *Return of the Living Dead III* on crack. If the situation wasn't so dire, I'd laugh my ass off. Though I knew it would only serve to piss the thing off.

"Jimmy, step away from there," Tabby said.

I turned to look back toward the window and felt myself tackled.

"Dammit, Jimmy." Tabby loomed over me. "The bitch was seeing you. We don't need her to know your face!"

"Too late now." Besides, I was used to screwing up. It was like my MO.

"Obviously, doofus."

I gently pushed against her. "Let me up."

Tabby rolled off me.

I got off the floor, but was careful to stay out of sight of the window.

"I think you should introduce me to your friends, Lulu. It's only polite."

The house buckled again. The floor in front of me cracked. This was not cool. Time was running out.

"This is really happening, isn't it?" Tabby asked me.

"Unfortunately, I think so."

"It's only going to hold for so long, Lulu. You have a choice to make," the voice outside said.

Woody stared at us. "We stay still. The house isn't bad yet."

The thing outside giggled. "How are you going to feel when you are nothing?"

Woody glared through the window. "I've already had nothing, you twit. I was born a slave. Nothing in my life has ever been as bad as that."

It cackled. "You haven't seen Hell yet."

Woody's eyes started to glow white. "That's where you're wrong. I've known Hell, and it ain't here."

The house rattled and the ceiling tiles in the living room started to fall. The house was trashed.

"All right, let's get moving," Woody said.

I swallowed hard. This was it. Time I bucked up and pretended to be brave.

Woody opened the back door. I could swear I heard suction release, like the sound when you opened a freezer.

"Ah, hiding no more, Lulu Woods," the thing said.

"I think the time for talking is over," Woody replied.

The thing stilled. "So be it."

It flung around a string of green power like a whip, and when it struck the house, sparks flew.

"Jesus Christ," I said and pushed Tabby behind me toward the other side of the house.

The thing cracked the whip again. Woody threw her hands apart and a beam of white light shot from her hands toward the thing. The thing danced away quickly.

It cracked its whip again and the end landed a mere six inches from my head. I ducked in time.

Woody lashed out with another beam of power and took one of the thing's legs. The plaster of the leg split and the body fell to the side. It laughed. Then, the ghost stepped out of its made body. Now, it resembled Doc and Lucy, but it was still covered in green light.

"I can always make another one," it said.

"It was the ugliest thing I ever saw anyway," I blurted out, then covered my mouth with my hand. Good job, dumbass.

The ghost snarled at me. "And who are you to speak to me?"

I stood up as straight as I could with all the bravado I could muster. "I'm Jimmy fucking Holiday, and that was my car."

Woody stared at me like I'd grown a set of horns or something. But this right here was exactly what I was good at.

The ghost flung her whip at me again, but this time, I caught it and held onto that string of power. Then, I started chanting. The crap that was coming out of my mouth was anything with a rhythm, song lyrics, plagiarized rhymes, crap like, "I like frogs, frogs like me, doodily, doodily, doodily, dee."

None of it seemed to matter. The intent mattered more than the words, and the important part was as long as I had hold of her, she could not attack anyone else.

Woody stared at me, looking like she couldn't believe what I was doing. The magic didn't hurt me. And it seemed to evaporate with my words. I couldn't hold this up forever though. I was running out of crap to chant.

I glanced at Tabby for help, but she stood there as speechless as Woody. I did the last thing I could think of. I pulled that woman's magic into prayer. I closed my eyes and concentrated on the sensation of drawing the power through me instead of into me. "God, help me, please. This needs to end and I don't know how."

The ghost began to scream.

I opened my eyes so I could watch her now that I could feel what needed to be done. "Dear Lord, this has been a tough few days, but I trust in you and your glory."

The ghost screamed again.

I stared up at the sky. "God, release this spirit. It does not know its time has come to an end."

The ghost screamed once more.

I stared down at it. The form trembled. "Dear Lord, give me the strength to bring this to an end. Bless us all, living and dead. Release the ones that no longer belong to this world. In Jesus' name, Amen."

I opened my hand and the ghost faded into nothingness. Her monstrous leg parts flapped on the ground, almost as if they were waiting on their owner.

"I sure hope Lucy doesn't want one of those," Tabby said.

Woody sighed. "You won't be having to worry about that."

I glanced over at her. "What are you talking about?"

She glanced back and forth between us. "You blessed them. You blessed us all."

I ran into the house. There was no Lucy. There was no Doc. I went into the living room and then I saw it. Doc's hat was sitting unceremoniously on the sofa all by itself.

I sank to the floor. My stupid fucking pride. I was such an idiot. My own lack of preparedness had taken them from me. I'd spoken without thinking, and it had been a disaster. They were gone.

"Where are they, Jimmy?" Tabby asked, shaken.

I stared off into space. "Gone."

"Gone where?"

I shrugged. "Wherever they are supposed to go. Doc would never leave his hat. They're gone."

"How could you?" She beat her hands against my back.

SEVENTEEN

NIGHT OF THE HUNTER

"MR. HOLIDAY!" a male voice yelled from outside.

I got up, pushed Tabby away, and headed into the kitchen, being careful not to trip over the crack in the floor. Woody watched as I walked, her back leaning against the kitchen counter.

Through the window, I could see him. He was about six feet tall with salt and pepper hair. He wore a black suit and a collar.

"Father Martin?" I asked loud enough so he could hear me.

"Yes, Mr. Holiday. I believe we have some unfinished business."

The hits kept coming. If I managed to survive without a nervous breakdown, then I would have accomplished something. "That might be an understatement."

"How many more people are going to get hurt before you quit this?" Woody asked me.

"I already tried to quit. He refused."

Woody gnashed her teeth. "The multiple attacks are getting old, and I can't help you much longer. Make a choice."

My life was in shambles. I'd accidentally wished away the spirits. Tabby hated me. I had nothing left except my own soul.

"What choice is there to make?" I asked her.

Woody glared at me. "You can give yourself up and see what will happen. Or you continue to fight and cherish what you have left."

None of it made any sense to me. I headed for the door. Either way, me going out there was going to accomplish something. I just didn't know what yet.

"Jimmy, no!"

I jerked around. Tabby stood in the doorway. Woody disappeared in a puff of smoke. It dawned on me then. Woody hadn't been back in the house with us. We'd been talking to an imposter. The whole few minutes had been so bad, I didn't realize Woody was more pissed off than usual. The wards were gone when the house broke. Woody was outside alone with that asshole.

A gunshot rang out.

I ran outside. Woody's body was lying at the bottom of the stairs, a single gunshot wound in the middle of her forehead.

My stomach felt like it hit the floor. This kind woman was gone. All because I hadn't been strong enough to prevent it. And it sucked. I swallowed the wetness that had started in my sinuses and I turned to the beast. "You sonofabitch."

He laughed. It sounded dark and old. I saw a flash of red flow across his eyes, then disappear.

"Father Martin, how long have you been possessed?"

He grinned. "My, my. Nothing gets by you, Mr. Holiday, does it?"

"Oh, plenty gets by me, but this is the first time I've gotten to see you in person. I'm used to looking for these signs. Again, how long have you been possessed?"

He flashed a malicious smile. "How long have you been alive?"

"Does the Order know?"

He leaned on the hood of my mangled car. "Do you have any idea how many of us are active within the church itself? Think of any evil thing that has happened in the name of the church and I can bet you that one of us is behind it."

I wanted to throw up. There was nothing I could do for Woody. Not now. All I could hope for was getting us out of there alive.

He motioned toward Woody's body. "You got rid of something of mine, it is only fair that I get rid of something of yours."

My shoulders tensed and I forced myself not to punch the shit out of him. "First of all, if I would have Marked the baby like you had asked, I hardly think it would have had the result you were hoping for."

He looked at me condescendingly. "It would have been under your power, thus, you would have been able to control it."

I cracked up. I couldn't help it. "You think I can control them? Seriously? One of them tried to kill me. I Mark them for God. That's it. He decides what to do with the soul. Literally, that's it."

He stared down his nose at me. "Oh, Mr. Holiday. You have no idea what you are capable of."

I closed my eyes and counted to ten. I wanted to avenge Woody's death. I wanted to say to heck with it and go home. I was tired of the games. And sadly, not all of these assholes got what they deserved. I had no safe place to exorcize him and he was way too strong and full of tricks for Tabby and me to tackle him and hold him down. We were so fucked.

I closed my eyes and reached my hands toward the sky. Winging an exorcism, even that was a new one for me. "Hail to the Guardians of the North, South, East, and West. Hear my call. Help God rid his servant of the demon or demons inhabiting his body. Release him now."

"You are too funny, Mr. Holiday. You don't even know my real name."

My eyes flashed to him. "I'm just getting started."

"Jimmy," I heard Tabby whisper. "Look down at the bottom of the door."

I glanced down. There was a small bottle of what I assumed was holy water sitting there. God bless her. I squatted and picked it up as fast as I could. The Father watched with an amused expression on his face. I flicked open the bottle of water and walked down the steps. I stopped when my feet hit Woody's body.

I flung the water into the shape of the cross onto him. "In the name of the Father, Son, and Holy Ghost, I cast you out, unclean spirit!"

He jerked up and stepped so close that he was almost standing on Woody. "It's going to take a lot more than that, Mr. Holiday."

He flung the water from his eyes as if he'd stepped out of a swimming pool. Then, he disappeared.

I glanced behind me, the car, under Woody's porch, but there was nothing.

"Tabby, help me," I whispered.

I arranged Woody's body under my arms and dragged her up the porch steps. Tabby stepped onto the porch.

"Get her legs, quick."

We carried her inside and set her on the floor. I kicked the kitchen door closed behind me. I wasn't sure if it would make any difference, but I had to try.

"What should we do?" Tabby asked.

"Let's put her in her bed where she would have been most comfortable. Then let's look in the spellroom to see if there is anything left in there we know how to use. Father Martin will show up again soon. I just don't know when."

"At least you do know one thing," she said.

"What's that?"

"You hurt him. And you must have done it pretty damn good or he wouldn't have needed to regroup."

"That's something, I guess. Would be better for shit to stop coming after us. This goes on much longer, and I'm going to have a heart attack."

"They say its bad news once the demons know who you are —they sure weren't kidding."

We went into the spellroom. I rifled through a few jars, but found nothing I knew how to use. I did grab a ceremonial knife. Not that I expected to get close enough to stab anything with it, but it made me feel better on some level to have a weapon I could see in my hands.

I left Tabby to her digging and wandered into the living room.

It was hard to believe this much had happened in such a short amount of time. No more Woody. No more Doc. No more Lucy. Either God was making plans for me to guard something big or evil was winning. At this point, I didn't know.

Suddenly, I knew someone was watching me. I glanced over to the picture window. Father Martin was standing there, his face pressed against the glass. Woody's wards must have been holding to some extent even after her death, but who know how long that would last. Why they held in one area and not in another I didn't know either. I didn't like all the unknown variables.

"Tabby," I said.

"Yeah?" she asked from the other room.

"Don't come out here. He's looking at me and I don't want him to see you."

I heard a couple of footsteps.

"Shit. Anything I can do?"

"Not right now. I think the wards are keeping him from coming inside. Be careful."

He stepped away from the window. I did not creep closer in case he threw a stone to break the window and get his hands on me, but there was nothing. It did occur to me that he was trying to freak me out.

"He's gone," I said, but I grabbed the curtains and pulled them shut. It wasn't a good risk to leave them open. Not anymore.

"Is it safe for me to come out now?"

"Into the living room at least. Kitchen, you should stay out of. The curtains on that window are worthless."

Tabby walked out of the hallway and gave me a hug.

"I'm getting tired."

She smoothed my hair. "I know you are. I am too."

"Promise me. If this turns south and I get turned into some type of monster, take me out."

She swatted me on the head lightly. "Now, why would I do that? You exorcized me."

I laid my forehead against hers. "And I'd do it again."

We stayed up all night. I stopped thinking I had hurt him that bad. He was gearing up for something else. I was sure of it. Every few minutes, Tabby would cross the room. I gave up telling her she should get off her feet a long time ago. We weren't doing that great emotionally, and the last thing we needed was to get into a fight.

"Shall we begin again, Mr. Holiday?"

I jumped.

Father Martin was standing in the doorway between the kitchen and the living room.

"Son of a bitch. Don't you ever give up?" I'd been right, the wards on the back side of the house had been broken. And if Tabby and I had had some sense, we would have tried to re-ward the place when we had the chance.

"Never."

I pushed Tabby behind me.

"While I'd seen the pictures of her, they did not do her justice," he said.

"Don't you talk to her. Don't you look at her. Don't you even think about her!"

He chuckled. "None of those are against the law, Mr. Holiday. I will do what I like."

"Back!" I put as much strength into my voice as possible.

His eyes grew wide and he staggered backward.

"Back. I'll say it again."

He stumbled further, his arms and legs twitching.

"You were not invited here. You were never invited here. As the emissary of Lulu Woods, I demand you to get out of this house!"

He flew backward through the kitchen door. Wood and glass splattered all over the porch. He landed on his back in the gravel. He slowly crawled to his feet and dusted the dirt off his back side. Then, he stared at me. "You see, Mr. Holiday. You are much stronger than you thought."

"None of this is about me. That's your biggest mistake."

"Come on, Mr. Holiday. Let's end this."

I took a deep breath and stepped onto the porch. "Father Martin, or whatever your name is, I exorcize you. Your kind does not belong here."

He laughed and threw his hand forward. My body slammed into the side of the house. I saw stars.

"Die, you motherfucking piece of pig shit." I stood up gingerly. "You aren't even worth the stress and strain. I've had enough of this."

"And what are you going to do about it?"

I sent as much power as I could muster free. "Be gone from my life, my sight, and my world, Martin. God revokes your invitation. Goodbye."

"Noooooooooo." His scream seemed to reach inside my skull and ring around like the sound of the bell notes before a church service.

Bright red light burst through every pore in his skin and gradually melded together until he was a mass of a humanoid blob. The red light got smaller and smaller as his voice faded. And finally, it winked out.

I stood there, holding my side, waiting for the next shoe to drop. When it didn't, I turned and started back into the house when I heard the sound of one person clapping.

I spun around.

There was the Devil, dressed in his fine black suit. He had a red handkerchief arranged in a diamond pattern in his pocket.

"And we meet again, Mr. Holiday."

EIGHTEEN
YEAR ZERO

"OH, FUCK ME," I said, leaning against the side of the house and not doing very good at holding it together.

The Devil smirked. "While I appreciate the offer, I'm afraid you are not my type."

"I'm not sure if I should be flattered or offended."

He chuckled. "With your sensibilities, be thoughtful. I don't think you could handle my cravings."

"Since you are here, I'm assuming we have something to discuss."

He smiled, showing a flash of fang. "Shall we have Tabby join us?"

There was a hiccup of light and Tabby was being held by the Devil, firmly.

"Let me go," she said.

"Come on now, play nice. I promise it will only hurt for a bit."

"Please, let her go," I said.

"Why would I do that? *She* is my type, Mr. Holiday. See, I told you to be thankful."

"Let me go," Tabby struggled against his grip, but did not make any progress.

"Don't fight. It's so much better if you don't fight." The Devil leaned down and kissed her neck. "I have to say, I'm quite impressed with your work, Mr. Holiday."

"Impressed or not, I think my ribs are broken and I knew better than to try to fight you." I ran a hand through my hair. I didn't dare attack the Devil. "I'd be a smear on the bottom of your shoe. Please, let her go."

"And what will you do for me, Mr. Holiday. There must be an exchange. Must keep the balance. You owe me."

"What are you talking about?" My eyes widened. I'd made no deal with him.

"You gave away my son."

Ezekiel. He did belong to Big Red. "And that idiotic yahoo wanted me to Mark him. I put him somewhere safe."

"That's the reason you and your pretty girl aren't dead right now. And before you say it, yes, I would risk God's wrath to kill you if you killed Ezekiel. He is capable of great things. But no matter. I will claim him. It will only take a little longer."

Tabby was trying to pry the Devil's fingers off her one by one. He snickered. "I like this one. She's feisty."

"Let her go. I don't want to die today."

The Devil clapped his hands together and grinned.

Tabby scurried away.

He lowered his hands and his eyes grew cold. "I'll let her go on one condition. You can become my Marker and I will set her free. Or you can continue working for Him and I'll make this pretty one my new plaything."

I collapsed onto the deck of the porch. The choice was impossible. Tabby kept looking back and forth between me and the Devil.

"Oh, and don't bother praying. He's preoccupied at the moment, trying to figure out how to get the soul of some that have been Marked released from Purgatory. Apparently, it is the first time that has happened."

He was so smug, it made me sick.

Tabby started to hyperventilate. I quietly prayed anyway, but nothing happened. I had tried.

"I don't have all day, Mr. Holiday. I need an answer."

I raised my eyebrow. "You have forever."

"While true, I do not feel like wasting forever standing here as you make up your mind. Choose."

Tabby glanced at me. Tears were pouring down her face.

"I'm sorry," I said to her. It was shitty and I knew it was wrong, but there was no right answer here. Both were wrong. Working for the Devil had consequences I had no way of knowing. Putting her into the pit with the ultimate high demon was awful. But it also did not mean the end of the world as we knew it. Or the world at large anyway. I was a shit and I was scared.

"You asshole!" Tabby spat at me.

The Devil grabbed her. "Nice doing business with you, Mr. Holiday." And he disappeared with Tabby in tow.

"Fuck!"

I fell back onto my butt and held my head in my hands. My mind flipped through all the times I'd had with her. Both good and bad. Her face. Her smell. The way she laughed when I did something stupid. And the way she held me when things went all ways wrong. I was such a piece of shit.

I staggered to my feet and wandered the grounds, but there was nothing for me there. I'd let him take her. Woody's corpse laid in the back room. Eventually, it would give way to dust. Tears poured down my face. I didn't bother to wipe them away. It wasn't like there was anyone to care what I did anymore.

Once I stopped crying, I wandered over to the car. It was not driveable. One tire in the front was pointed east and the other was pointed west. I kicked the tire nearest to me and hurt my foot. There was nothing left for me to do but go home and regroup. Or find someone to fix this mess. Who was I kidding? I didn't know what I was doing.

I took a deep breath and stared up at the sky. Wasn't one damn cloud. It should have been storming. But there was no sign that anything bad had happened there except the marks in the grass. Those would be gone as the grass grew. Like my life.

When I went inside the house, I called for Isaac. No answer. I hollered again and waited. He never came. I wandered through all the rooms, but he was gone. He either followed Tabby into the underworld because he was her familiar or he ran away. I had no way of knowing.

I even dug through the bottom of all the closets in the house. He was not there. I waited around for a couple more hours in case he came back, but he never did.

I grabbed some clothes from my suitcase and put them in a garbage bag. It was a heck of a lot lighter for me to carry. I didn't need much now. No telling how long I was going to have to hoof it. I made sure to get my phone and charger, and I hobbled down the hill. I was so technologically stupid, I didn't even know how to get that Uber thing to work. Hitchhiking it was. Luckily my non-Order credit cards were paid up. I doubted if my black card worked.

When I got to the main road, I stuck out my thumb and started walking backward into the sun.

Thank you for reading! Did you enjoy? Please add your review because nothing helps an author more and encourages readers to take a chance on a book than a review.

And don't miss the next book of the *The Marker Chronicles,* SORROW'S FALL, coming soon. Until then, check out the Author's Note regarding Woody on the next page.

And then, find your next read, SUPERSTITION, by James Blakey. Turn the page for a sneak peek!

You can also sign up for the City Owl Press newsletter to receive notice of all book releases!

AUTHOR'S NOTE

Woody was real…

Lulu "Woody" Woods was my father's godmother. My father grew up in the coal camps of West Virgina, and life was hard for everybody. Woody always had him and his siblings come visit. Her own son was long out of the house, so she was an extra grandmother to my dad and my aunts and uncle. Apparently, she had the best sugar cookies ever. She always served the cookies with giant scoops of vanilla ice cream. There was a fight with an evil witch who gave birth to a devil baby in the camp. The devil baby was taken away by priests who came down from Pittsburgh, PA, or so the story goes. This was supposed to have happened in the late 1940s or early 1950s. Woody lived until the 1970s. My dad has kept her alive all these years talking about how kind she was and the spiritual songs she would sing. And she did chase the evil witch with a chicken's foot.

SNEAK PEEK OF SUPERSTITION
BY JAMES BLAKEY

WEDNESDAY 3:55PM

Darla Jaggard's calves burned as she dashed up the concrete steps two at a time. The air was unusually warm for early autumn in upstate New York, and perspiration trickled down her back. Behind her, three trima figures in shiny green-and-gold warm-up suits, carrying matching gym bags, struggled to keep pace.

"Last one to the top is a rotten egg!" With a burst of speed, Darla, her honey-blonde hair secured with red ribbons, pulled away from the others. Two older brothers and a beauty queen mother made life a contest for as long as she could remember.

Descending students, coeds with a glare in their eyes, boys twisting their necks to watch, hustled to one side for fear of being run over.

Darla reached the top, tossed her bag, planted her feet, and launched into a backflip. Knees tucked tight to her body, she spun like a pinwheel and nailed a perfect landing. Flashing the smile of an Olympic champion gracing a box of breakfast cereal, she raised her arms in a V and announced, "I win." Her green eyes grew wide, and a frown replaced her smile. "You split the group!" She pointed an accusing finger at Cassie McGlaughlin.

Cassie, a dark-haired freshman and last of the four girls, slowed as she approached the top step and dropped her bag. "What are you talking about?" She leaned over, hands on knees, catching her breath.

"You ran up the other side." Darla pointed to the rusty metal railing dividing the steps. "The three of us were on this side."

Darla sneered and crossed her arms. The other two girls, Talia and Veronica, flanked Darla, striking identical poses hands on their hips, auburn hair pulled back, hazel eyes narrowed, and lips pressed into thin lines.

"And?" Cassie arched an eyebrow.

Darla let out an exaggerated sigh. "Everyone knows that's bad luck. Worse than taking a selfie with a black cat. Who knows what could happen? We might not get a bid for Dallas or lose a sponsor." Her eyes sparkled as she concocted the solution. "Unless you go back down and run up our side." She made a walking motion with her fingers.

Talia and Veronica nodded in simultaneous agreement, as if Darla's brain controlled both girls' actions.

Clouds darkened the sky, and a few scattered raindrops fell.

"Where do you come up with all these nutty ideas?" Cassie shook her head, "You're all delusional, and we're late. Coach isn't going to be happy." She picked up her gym bag. "If you think it's such a big deal, why don't you and the *Olsen twins* run back down and come up my side?" She stuck out her tongue, turned, and disappeared through the glass double doors of the gymnasium.

Darla's face reddened. "Sometimes she can be such a b—"

Inside the poorly lit gymnasium, a single faded banner hung from the rafters: Van Buren University Men's Basketball — 1947 Presidential Conference Champions. The ancient air-conditioning system rattled loudly as if to announce it wasn't dead, while circulating muggy air filled with the scent of bubble gum, cherry lip gloss, and sweat.

Marcus Reed, six-four with dark, curly hair, stood on the

ratty black safety mat covering a third of the basketball court. He supported Cassie with a muscular arm and a sturdy hand. With a plastic smile, she leaned forward and raised her right leg, her body contorting into a capital *T*. She counted five, her body becoming more unsteady with each number. As she shakily returned to an upright position, Marcus's arm collapsed. Cassie tumbled through the air, but Marcus recovered, grunting as she landed in his arms.

Nearby, twenty-five other cheerleaders in T-shirts and shorts practiced tosses, leaps, and flips. A few girls stretched on the mat, gossiping or scrolling through phones. Heavy rain pounded the gymnasium roof. A couple guys placed buckets to catch the water dripping from the ceiling.

Coach Erica Nightlinger, her mousy brown hair pulled back in a perpetual ponytail, observed her squad. Perhaps half the boys were on performance enhancers, while a third of the girls could have eating disorders. She hadn't specifically encouraged her team to endanger their health through drugs and starvation, but she did turn a blind eye. According to the rumblings from the Athletic Department, this was her last year unless she brought home a championship. If she couldn't transform this third-rate cheer team into a contender, Nightlinger would be back to teaching dance in strip malls to uncoordinated tweens and their helicopter mothers.

"Okay, let's bring it in. Stragglers too!" She waved at the three late arrivals running penalty laps around the perimeter.

The team assembled on the mat in a semi-circle facing Nightlinger.

"It's less than a month until Nationals. We can't let up now. No matter how hard you're trying, no matter how sore, how tired, you can always give more. Here's proof." She held up her left hand to display a gold championship ring. "I wear this ring every day to remind myself of what I've accomplished. You can achieve this, too, if you make the commitment."

The truth was that Nightlinger bought the ring off eBay. The

year that Lyndon Johnson State won the National Championship, she was on academic probation. Too many late nights at
Smokey Joe's combined with eight a.m. Intro to Statistics.

She raised her hand over head. "Do you want this?"

"Yes!" the squad replied in chorus.

"Again, louder. Do you want this?"

"Yes!" The answer echoed throughout the gym.

"Better! And if necessary, I'll put myself in there. And you
know I will."

That elicited a round of nervous laughter from the squad.
Within a pound or two of her cheer weight, Nightlinger would
insert herself into the practices when the squad floundered. In
moments of desperation, she would concoct schemes where she
assumed the identity of one of the girls, placing herself on the
squad when they competed at Nationals.

"Circle up." The coach made a clockwise motion with
her arm.

The squad formed a ring, their right hands touching in the
center. "One, two, three! Statesmen!"

"Let's do this." Nightlinger pointed at her squad. "Arms
straight and no boring faces."

The cheerleaders struck poses and displayed a series of
winks, open mouths, and dropped jaws.

Nightlinger pressed play on the ancient boombox, and
static crackled at maximum volume. Cheerleaders covered
their ears. She fiddled with the device for a few moments
before giving up. "Who's got a phone with the playlist that I
can borrow?"

A brunette tossed her iPhone to the coach. Nightlinger
hooked up the phone to the sound system and pressed play.
High-energy techno-jazz boomed from the sound system,
echoing throughout the gym.

Girls leapt, spun, and bounced into back flips. Marcus and
another boy locked their wrists to form a basket. Cassie hopped
into the basket, steadying herself on their shoulders. Two spot-

ters placed their hands under the others. With a mighty effort, the four propelled her twenty feet into the air.

At the apex, Cassie split her legs, touching her toes. She descended toward waiting arms. A deafening roar of thunder filled the gymnasium, and the lights flickered. In the momentary darkness, her foot collided with someone's head, redirecting her fall. Marcus scrambled to catch her, but Cassie slammed to the floor, eating mat.

The rest of the team continued performing basket catches, rewinds, and liberties. The routine slowly came to a standstill as the squad realized something was amiss. Cassie lay motionless on the mat.

"Why is everybody stopping?" Nightlinger threw up her hands. "McGlaughlin, you go down like that in Dallas, you better not lie there. You get hurt, you roll off."

The squad made a half-hearted attempt to pick up the performance while Cassie remained unmoving. Nightlinger blew her whistle and killed the music. She walked over and knelt by Cassie, who had managed to sit up. The girl moved her jaw, wheezing, but no words were forthcoming.

Nightlinger placed a hand on the cheerleader's shoulder. "Take it easy. You got the wind knocked out of you." She shouted at her team, "Everyone, you have two minutes. Grab a drink!"

A variety of water bottles, electrolyte replacements, and energy drinks were retrieved from gym bags and guzzled.

Cassie gasped until her breathing returned to normal. A blank look crossed her face. "What happened, did I fall?"

Nightlinger looked around at the squad. "Anyone see? Did she hit her head?" The question was met by shrugs and stares. She pointed an accusing finger at Marcus. "You should have caught her. You're better than that."

Marcus shrugged. "But Coach, the lights went out."

"*But Coach, the lights went out,*" Nightlinger mocked. "We've been rehearsing this routine for weeks. You should be able to do it blindfolded." She dismissed Marcus with a wave of her hand. "Rokozny." The coach pointed at a strawberry-blonde stunter. "Go find a trainer."

The girl scampered off through a side entrance.

Ridiculous, thought Nightlinger. *The basketball team gets three trainers and God knows how many assistants, for half as many athletes, while I get less than nothing for the most dangerous sport on campus. Someday, we're going to get sued. And I'll be there to say 'I told you so.' If I'm not fired first.*

"I'll watch her, Coach." Marcus offered Cassie a hand and lifted her to her feet. "Lean on me." Even using Marcus for support, Cassie wobbled. "I have an idea." He reached behind her knees and hefted her up.

Secure in his arms, Cassie locked her hands around Marcus's neck, pulled their faces closer, and gazed into his sky-blue eyes. "My hero."

Nightlinger observed the goofy grins on both their faces. Last thing her team needed was romantic complications sparking jealousy among the rest of the squad, then the harsh feelings between Cassie and Marcus after the inevitable break-up. The coach would stop this budding flirtation before it destroyed her team. She followed Marcus across the court to the bleachers.

He gently placed Cassie in the first row, then sat next to her and held her hand. "Okay?"

"Yeah, I think so." Cassie squeezed his hand. Music again filled the gym, and the cheerleaders resumed their routine. "You should probably join the squad."

"Nah, I've got to keep an eye on our number one flyer."

"Uh, uh." Nightlinger pointed at Marcus. "You need to get in there. And no more mistakes."

"Okay." Marcus squeezed Cassie's hand once more, then jogged over to the other cheerleaders and resumed his place in the routine.

"You're going to be okay." Nightlinger sat next to Cassie. "Here comes help."

Skip Stetter, one of the basketball team trainers, jogged across the court. He wore a green VBU polo and khakis. In his right hand, he carried a med kit. He knelt next to Cassie and pulled a laminated 8.5" x 11" sheet from his bag.

"What happened, did I fall?" Cassie said again.

Skip searched for the concussion protocols on the sheet.

"Don't you know what to do?" Nightlinger stared at Skip.

Skip stared at the instructions. "This is very technical. I don't want to get it wrong."

"What happened, did I fall?"

"She keeps asking the same thing," Nightlinger slumped her shoulders. "She got the wind knocked out of her. No one's sure if she hit her head or what."

"Just let me do this." Skip grabbed Cassie's wrist, felt for a pulse, and checked his watch. "Fifty-two beats per minute. An athlete's heart." He released her wrist. "I'm going to ask you a few questions. Can you tell me your name?"

"Cassie." Her tone implied everyone should know it.

"Very good, Cassie. And do you know what day of the week it is?"

"It's Wednesday." She squinted at him. "Why?"

"These are the questions on the sheet. And where are you?"

She sighed. "Van Buren U. In the gym."

"Very good. Three for three."

"Is she going to be all right?" Nightlinger leaned forward trying to read the sheet in Skip's hands.

"Have to check a few more things." Skip reached into his bag for a penlight and aimed the beam into Cassie's brown eyes. Her pupils shrank to the size of pinheads. "Cassie, I want you to follow the light with your eyes while keeping your head still." He motioned the pen to the left, then back to the right.

Cassie's eyes didn't move. She stared straight ahead.

He leaned closer. "Cassie, can you hear me?"

"What happened, did I fall?"

Skip waved the pen in front of her face. "I want you to follow the light with your eyes."

"What light? Everything just went black." Her body shuddered. "I can't see!"

He clicked off the penlight. "Are you sure?"

"Yes, I'm sure! How could I not be?" she screamed, then broke into tears.

Nightlinger wrapped her arms around Cassie in a tight hug. "Everything's going to be okay," she whispered.

Skip pulled out his phone. "I better call 9-1-1."

Don't stop now. Keep reading with your copy of
SUPERSTITION.

And sign up for Danielle's newsletter to get all the news,
giveaways, excerpts, and more!

Don't miss book five in the *The Marker Chronicles*, SORROW'S LIE, coming soon, and find more from Danielle DeVor at www.danielledevor.com

Until then, find your next read, SUPERSTITION, by City Owl author, James Blakey

An umbrella is opened indoors. A black cat crosses your path. Three cigarettes are lit from one match. These are omens of bad luck that no one takes seriously. But at Van Buren University when these, and other superstitions, are broken... students die.

Sophomore Jerry Williams' hard-hitting reporting has won awards for Van Buren's school newspaper. But when he connects a series of campus deaths to bad luck, his editor questions Jerry's judgment, kills the story, and suspends him from the paper. But the superstition-related havoc continues, and Darla, Jerry's new girlfriend, barely escapes with her life.

When Jerry digs deeper into the mystery and publishes his findings in the school's alternative newspaper, the university administration threatens him with suspension for causing a panic. But Jerry's reporting instincts won't let him stop. With his friends and everyone else on campus at risk, it's not like Jerry has much of a choice.

As Friday the 13th approaches, Jerry fears a catastrophe. He must uncover who—or what—is behind these bad luck deaths and determine how to stop it.

All reviews are **welcome** and **appreciated**. Please consider leaving one on your favorite social media and book buying sites.

Escape Your World. Get Lost in Ours! City Owl Press at www.cityowlpress.com

ACKNOWLEDGMENTS

First of all, I would like to thank Tina Moss for not only being an amazing editor, but for being an awesome friend as well. Then, comes Tabatha Barber for being an awesome friend, beta reader, and for letting me borrow her cat. Josh Devor, for being a great cousin and for meticulously buying all my books. My folks, for giving me the support to do this. Kristin Dutt, for the many "Jared" gif sessions on FB. Julia Long, for being there. :) And, above all else, my fans, the Devorkians, for following Jimmy blindly into the darkness.

ABOUT THE AUTHOR

Danielle DeVor is the author of many spooky things including, The Marker Chronicles: *Exorcisms or bust. Half price offer. The exorcisms, not the book. Jimmy will exorcise you for a fee. Just call him;* Maw: *Space Vampires, woo;* and other ramblings. She's won awards, yay, *Examiner's list of Women in Horror: 93 Horror Authors You Need to Read Right Now.* Her pet iguana, Sam,  has since passed into the ether, living with vampires in a big house where they feed him treats everyday. She wears a lot of black and listens to some pretty out there music, talking your ear off about Motionless in White and Type O Negative. *Beware.* And she loves anything horror or monster-y. *No, that isn't a word. But it's more fun than saying monstrous. Bite her.*

www.danielledevor.com

facebook.com/danielle.devor
x.com/sammyig
instagram.com/danielledevor76

ABOUT THE PUBLISHER

City Owl Press is a cutting edge indie publishing company, bringing the world of romance and speculative fiction to discerning readers.

Escape Your World. Get Lost in Ours!

www.cityowlpress.com

facebook.com/CityOwlPress
x.com/cityowlpress
instagram.com/cityowlbooks
pinterest.com/cityowlpress
tiktok.com/@cityowlpress